2
VOYAGERS

GAME OF FLAMES

Robin Wasserman

Random House New York

Copyright © 2015 by PC Studios Inc.
Full-color interior art, puzzles, and codes copyright © Animal Repair Shop
Voyagers digital and gaming experience by Animal Repair Shop

All rights reserved. Published in the United States by
Random House Children's Books,
a division of Penguin Random House LLC, New York.

Random House and the colophon are registered trademarks of
Penguin Random House LLC.

Visit us on the Web! randomhousekids.com

Educators and librarians, for a variety of teaching tools,
visit us at RHTeachersLibrarians.com

VoyagersHQ.com

Library of Congress Cataloging-in-Publication Data
Wasserman, Robin.
Game of flames / Robin Wasserman.—First edition.
pages cm.—(Voyagers ; book 2)
Summary: Dash, Carly, Gabriel, and Piper visit a planet made up of
molten lava and run entirely by robots where they must find the second
element of the Source that will save the Earth.
ISBN 978-0-385-38661-6 (trade)—ISBN 978-0-385-38663-0 (lib. bdg.)—
ISBN 978-0-385-38662-3 (ebook)
[1. Interplanetary voyages—Fiction. 2. Human-alien encounters—Fiction.
3. Power resources—Fiction. 4. Science fiction.] I. Title.
PZ7.W25865Gam 2015
[Fic]—dc23
2014041650

Printed in the United States of America
10 9 8 7 6 5 4 3 2 1
First Edition

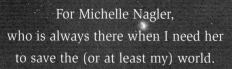

For Michelle Nagler,
who is always there when I need her
to save the (or at least my) world.
—R.W.

Deep in the heart of an ancient jungle, hundreds of light-years from Earth, an engine roared to life. Moments later, a sleek silver ship lifted from the ground. It shot up over the towering trees and sliced through the clouds, a spear of light. The jungle growled and chittered and screeched at the unnatural sight. Raptogons threw back their heads, bared their teeth, and shrieked at the sky. The ship rocketed up and up, a rising star that blazed sharp and bright . . . and then was gone.

In its wake, a blanket of silence dropped over the jungle. Only the quiet chirping of birds and buzzing of insects disturbed the stillness.

Until . . . footsteps.

A boy stepped out of his hiding place in the trees.

A boy who did not belong on this planet, any more than the crew of the silver ship had.

A boy with a ship of his own.

He was dressed all in black, with an omega symbol emblazoned on his right shoulder. He tilted his head to the sky, as if to make sure that the ship was really gone. That he was finally alone.

He had watched from the shadows as the three humans wrestled the gigantic Raptogon. He had half expected the hundred-and-fifty-foot lizard to swallow them whole.

That would have been just fine with him.

Instead, they'd done the impossible. They had yanked a tooth from the furious creature and escaped with their lives. They had taken part of it back to their ship, where they would crush it into powder. Rapident Powder was one of six elements that, when put together, would create a clean, self-sustaining source of power. It would save the Earth, which had almost no power left.

This crew risked everything to scour the universe for all six elements. The boy had watched them celebrate finding the first one.

Of course, they didn't know he was there.

There was so much they didn't know.

Whereas he knew everything.

Dash Conroy, Piper Williams, Gabriel Parker—those were their names. Carly Diamond had guided their movements from their home ship, the *Cloud Leopard*. And, finally, there was the one named Chris, who they thought they could trust.

The Voyagers.

The Alpha team, they proudly called themselves. As if being first made them special.

The boy knew this about them, along with everything else that mattered. While they knew nothing about him— they didn't even know he existed. Or that he had followed them.

If they had known, surely they wouldn't have left part of the Raptogon tooth behind.

The boy padded across the mossy jungle floor and stooped to examine the remaining piece of tooth. It was the size of a door and streaked with dried Raptogon spit. He allowed himself a small smile. Yes, this would work just fine. He raised his left hand and pressed the touch screen that fitted across the back of his hand like a claw. In the distance, another engine powered up, responding to his signal. He waited impatiently for his transport shuttle to speed its way through the jungle toward him. He was eager to get back to his home ship—there was no time to waste. At any moment, the *Cloud Leopard* might shift into Gamma Speed. When it did, he would be right behind them.

The boy had been hiding, waiting, following for a long time.

He was tired of it.

Soon, he thought, it would be time to reveal himself. To show these Alphas who they were up against. It didn't matter anymore if they knew he was following them. They couldn't stop him. Because he knew something else they didn't: even when you were following someone, you could still be one step ahead.

Dash Conroy studied the touch screen beside the portal, tracing his finger along the route he'd mapped out. Each symbol marked a different junction in the vast, tangled nest of tubes that wove through the ship. A single wrong move, and everything would be lost. He was the Alpha team leader, responsible for everything that happened on board the *Cloud Leopard* and this mission—he couldn't afford to make mistakes.

He checked the route.

He double-checked it.

Perfect.

Dash tapped the screen, finalizing the input. Then he wrapped his hands around the horizontal metal bar installed above the portal.

This was it.

Moment of truth.

He took a deep breath and swung himself off his feet and into the tube. A gush of air swept him into motion, speeding him toward the heart of the *Cloud Leopard.*

"Woooooooooooo!" Dash whooped, but the wind stole his scream away. He flew through gleaming tunnels, powerless to stop himself, even if he wanted to. Up and up at breakneck speed, then a sharp left into a branching tube, down so fast and so steep his stomach leapt into his throat. It was like the world's wildest waterslide, except instead of sputtering through freezing water, he was surfing a cushion of warm air. Dash veered right. He zoomed through one loop-the-loop, then another, plunged down another sharp drop, and shot out of the tube like a cannonball. He landed with a thud exactly where he'd planned, on the lower level of the ship's training center.

Mission accomplished.

"Woo-hoo!" Dash cheered when he checked his time. One minute, two seconds. A new ship record. Three miles of tubing made for thousands of different routes through the ship and the crew was competing to see who could find the longest one. Carly had managed fifty-two seconds on her last run—Dash had spent hours trying to beat her. He clasped his hands over his head like a prizefighter. "Victory is mine!"

Yes, Dash was the team leader on an interstellar mission hurtling through space at speeds faster than light. Yes, he had the most important job in the world—maybe the galaxy. And that one job was actually more like four: Piper was the ship medic, Carly was the science and tech officer, Gabriel was the navigator and pilot—and Dash had to know everything they did. Just in case.

In the fifty-five days since they'd left planet J-16, he'd had plenty of important things to do: memorizing ship schematics, practicing in the flight simulator, studying up on their next destination, the planet Meta Prime.

But Dash had his priorities straight: he always made time for tube surfing.

"One minute, two seconds!" he called out. "Ship record, for sure! *Yesss.*"

"Watch out next time!" Piper cried. "You almost landed on some ZRKs!"

"What?" Dash suddenly realized he was surrounded by a cloud of tiny, golf ball–sized machines. They were buzzing like a hive of angry bees. Or like a hive of miniature robots he'd almost sat on. "Uh, sorry, little guys."

The *Cloud Leopard* couldn't function without its fleet of tiny ZRKs. The clever robots prepped mission tech, repaired damage to the ship, and did anything else the crew might need. They were also pretty good at getting in the way.

"Remember, ZRKs are people too," Piper said. She was nowhere in sight. "Well, not technically."

"Not at all actually," Dash pointed out. He looked around for the source of Piper's voice but couldn't find her. "Where are you, anyway?"

"Up here!" Piper shouted.

Dash looked up.

Way, way up.

The training center was an enormous atrium, two

stories high. And sure enough, there was Piper, hovering above a catwalk, nearly a hundred feet off the ground. Piper grinned and waved down at him. The catwalk was less than two feet wide, but Piper didn't look too worried. She knew she couldn't fall. Her air chair wouldn't let her.

Until she was five years old, Piper was just like any other kid. Then came the accident.

She could still remember how it felt when they told her she would never walk again.

She could still remember how it felt to walk, because she did so in her dreams.

Piper told herself it didn't matter. She was just as smart as other kids, just as brave, just as capable. Hadn't she proven it by getting chosen for this mission? Thousands of kids from everywhere on Earth had tried for a spot on this ship—the smartest, toughest kids the world had to offer. And out of all of them, the people in charge had picked *her*.

The best part of the mission was getting the chance to save the world. But the second best part was definitely her brand-new, custom-built hovercraft wheelchair. Who cared whether or not she could walk? Now she could fly!

She'd spent all morning zipping around the upper level of the training center watching the ZRKs at work and the rest of the crew at play. The tubes may have been fun, but they couldn't compare to her air chair.

"A new ship's record!" Dash cheered himself again, heading across the training room toward Gabriel and

Carly, who'd taken over the basketball court. Neither of them noticed. For weeks, Gabriel and Carly had been complaining about their training regimen. They were getting bored, doing the same exercises every single day. So STEAM 6000, the ship's robot, had come up with something different.

STEAM designed a virtual reality training game, just for them. It seemed to be some combination of basketball, fencing, lacrosse, and juggling fire. Dash didn't quite understand the rules, but Carly and Gabriel had been at it for days. They wore thick black virtual reality glasses, and ducked and weaved around virtual fireballs and digital lightning bolts that no one else could see.

They looked totally ridiculous. But Dash kept that opinion to himself.

"Don't you guys ever sleep?" he asked them from the safety of the sidelines.

Carly ducked, then jumped over some invisible hurdle. She kicked out her right leg, then grunted as if something had whacked her in the stomach. "Can't sleep," she gasped. "Too busy winning."

"You must be asleep now," Gabriel jeered as he slid to the ground and wrapped his hands around an invisible ball. He slammed it back toward Carly. "Because you're *dreaming.*"

"What's the score?" Dash asked.

"Where are we, Steamer?" Carly asked.

The training robot didn't hesitate. "The score is

62,094 to 61,997, in favor of Carly, yes sir! She's beating him like a drum, she is!"

"In your *face!*" Carly squealed, just as Gabriel launched a barrage of something at her head. Dash swallowed a laugh.

"Now 62,098 to 62,094 in favor of Gabriel," STEAM corrected itself. "He is the king of the world, he is!"

Carly grimaced. She liked Gabriel, but she loved winning. "You're going down, Gabe," she said.

Dash grinned at his crew. No one would guess these were two of the smartest twelve-year-olds on Earth—or that the fate of the planet was in their hands.

It was easy, at times like this, to forget about their mission. To forget that they couldn't make it back home without retrieving all six of the elements, and if they failed, they would be stranded. Lost in space forever, while the people of Earth slowly ran out of fuel and energy, until the whole planet went dark.

Sometimes, it was good to forget. To revel in the fact that he was on a state-of-the-art spaceship equipped with Ping-Pong tables and a digital copy of every movie ever made. But it was also times like that, the fun times, when he missed his family the most. His mother and his little sister, Abby, were all alone back in Orlando. He imagined them staring out at the city gone dark, every light powered down for the energy curfew. Or maybe they were gazing up at the stars, wondering when he would come home. If he would come home.

Dash was proud to lead this mission—to risk everything to save his family and his planet.

But deep down, he was terrified he wouldn't be able to do it.

It amazed him that he could stuff so many opposing feelings into his brain at the same time. It was smaller than a football in there—how could there be room for them all?

STEAM suddenly *eep*ed in alarm. "No time for games anymore!"

"One more serve," Carly complained. "I've got him this time, I know it."

"Check yourself before you wreck yourself," STEAM said excitedly. Dash groaned. The robot might be the most advanced piece of human technology ever made, but sometimes it sounded more like the star of a lame old TV sitcom. "I have word from the navigation deck, we're exiting Gamma Speed."

Dash snapped into commander mode. "Exiting Gamma Speed!" he called up to Piper. "All crew to the bridge!"

"Yes, sir." Gabriel saluted, winking at him. Gabriel was still getting used to the idea that Dash could tell him what to do. Teasing him about it helped.

Usually.

"Let's go!" Carly said, racing the others to the tube portal as Chris's voice echoed throughout the ship.

"All crew members, please report to the navigation deck," he said. "Exiting Gamma Speed imminently."

"Tell us something we don't know," Gabriel said, and leapt into the tube after Carly.

Chris was the fifth member of their crew. He was a few years older and spent most of his free time by himself. Dash and the others didn't know much about where he'd come from or how he'd ended up on the *Cloud Leopard*. Unlike the rest of them, Chris hadn't had to compete for a spot. Commander Shawn Phillips, the leader of Project Alpha, had simply assigned him to the ship.

And he did it *without* telling the other members of the crew.

It had taken Gabriel some time to get used to that too—and he wasn't the only one. Chris was supposedly some kind of super-genius who'd helped design the Voyagers' mission. Which meant he knew things about it the others didn't. And no one liked being in the dark.

One by one, the crew whooshed through the tubes toward the fore of the ship, popping out on the bridge. Piper skimmed her air chair down the central corridor and met them on the flight deck a few seconds later. The enormous, wraparound window showed a sky streaked with shimmers of light. At Gamma Speed, stars didn't look like stars. More like ribbons of luminescence, wrapping and spiraling around the *Cloud Leopard* at wild speeds. It made Dash dizzy to look at them, but he could never force himself to look away.

"Ready?" Dash asked his crew as they assembled on the flight deck. A shiver of excitement ran down his spine. The ship exited Gamma Speed on autopilot—all they needed to do was strap in and prepare to enter orbit. That is, unless something went wrong.

Dash was always prepared for something to go wrong.

"Ready," they said in unison. The four members of the Alpha crew strapped themselves into the flight seats lined up before the controls. Traveling at Gamma Speed felt the same as standing still, and once the ship was in orbit, the ship's artificial gravity system would kick in. But getting from one to the other took a little getting used to.

It also took a pretty tough seat belt.

Gabriel slipped on the dark flight glasses that would let him take manual control of the ship once they entered Meta Prime's orbit.

Chris had his own flight seat in his private quarters, but he'd opened up a comm line with the bridge. "Ready from here," he reported.

"Prepare to exit Gamma Speed," the computer warned.

Dash gripped the edges of his flight chair. The ship shook and heaved. Massive g-forces flattened him against the seat. The force of deceleration rattled his teeth and made his skin feel like it was melting off his face.

"I-I-I-I-I ha-a-a-a-a-ate thi-i-i-i-i-i-i-is pa-a-a-a-a-rt!" Carly complained through clattering teeth.

The others couldn't answer—they were trying too hard not to be sick.

The pressure intensified. Dash wondered how flat he could get before he turned two-dimensional. Or before his brain melted out of his ears. Then, just when he couldn't take it a single second longer—

It was over.

Gravity returned to normal. Or, at least, artificial normal. The ship stopped shaking, the engines stopped roaring, Gabriel shifted them into a stable orbit, everything was totally fine. Exactly as it was supposed to be. Except . . .

"Uh, guys, am I seeing things?" Gabriel asked, taking off his flight glasses and pointing a shaky finger at the window, which, only seconds ago, had looked out at a starry stretch of empty space. "Or is that . . . ?"

"Mass hallucination?" Carly suggested hopefully. "Some kind of side effect of Gamma Speed they didn't tell us about?"

"It's really there," Piper said, chewing on her lip. "But I don't see how it's possible. Dash? What do you think?"

Dash said nothing. Only gaped at the view, eyes wide. He blinked hard as if to clear his vision.

It didn't work.

Something was materializing in space before his eyes, something huge that blotted out the stars.

And that something was another ship.

3

The navigation deck exploded with confusion.

"What is that?"

"*Who* is that?"

"How can there be anyone else out here?"

"Are they following us?"

"Who *are* they?"

Voices overlapped, all of them tinged with panic. They were hundreds of light-years away from home, hurtling through the vast emptiness of space. It was impossible that they would just happen to cross paths with another ship.

And yet . . .

There it was, a dark, hulking ship, about the same size as the *Cloud Leopard*. Where the *Cloud Leopard* was all graceful sloping curves, this ship was straight lines and sharp angles, like an arrow slicing through the fabric of space. But there was still something familiar about it. Something niggling at the back of Dash's mind.

Something about the two ships that made them feel like a matched pair.

Chris appeared on the bridge within seconds. He looked just as shocked as everyone else.

"Did you know about this?" Dash asked him, even though the answer was written across his face. "Another ship?"

Chris shook his head. Even though Dash still had questions about how Chris ended up on their mission, he'd come to rely on the older boy as a source of steadiness and guidance. There was something comforting about having his knowledge on board. It was unsettling to see him so confused.

"What do we do if they try to fire on us?" Gabriel asked. "Shouldn't we be, like, readying the photon torpedoes?"

"A photon torpedo is a physical impossibility," Chris said, sounding puzzled.

"Okay, how about a laser cannon?" Gabriel tried. "There must be some kind of laser cannon. In case we find a Death Star or something."

"This isn't a movie," Carly said wearily. "There aren't any Death Stars. Or Klingons. Or laser cannons."

"Why are we even talking about shooting at them?" Piper said. "They haven't done anything."

"*Yet*," Gabriel said meaningfully.

"Shouldn't we find out who they are?" Piper insisted.

"And what exactly they're doing out here?"

"Definitely," Dash agreed. "Let's open up a channel of communication with them." Then he turned uncertainly to Chris. "Uh, we can do that, right?"

"We can certainly try," Chris said. "There's no guarantee they'll answer."

Carly, who'd studied every inch of the ship, including the communication system, took the controls. She chose a wide-band frequency, then gave Dash a sharp nod.

Dash cleared his throat. He stared into the pin-sized camera that would beam his image to the other ship. "This is Dash Conroy, on the *Cloud Leopard,* leader of the Alpha team. We're on a mission from Earth. We . . . uh . . ." He searched for something impressive and leader-like to say. "We come in peace."

Behind him, Gabriel snorted.

There was a long moment of silence. Then an image appeared on the giant monitor overhead, revealing the inside of a ship—and a girl's face.

A face Dash had come to know extremely well. One he thought he would never see again.

Or at least, hoped he would never see again.

"You?" he said.

Anna Turner, who he'd beaten out for mission leader, gave him a wicked grin. "Me."

Back on Earth, at Base Ten, Anna and Dash had competed side by side for weeks. Anna was bossy, selfish, hot-tempered, and determined to win at all costs. Dash would never forget the look on her face when she found out she'd lost. That she would have to return home, a failure. That there would be no mission, no ten-million-dollar prize money, no intergalactic adventure for her.

Except that here she was, in a spaceship of her own. So maybe she hadn't lost after all? Dash had never been so confused.

Anna's grin widened. "And not just me. Meet the crew of the *Light Blade.*"

At her words, the view on the monitor expanded to reveal the rest of her crew. Dash couldn't believe it. None of the Alpha team could. Strapped into flight chairs on this strangely familiar ship's bridge were all four of the other finalists for Project Alpha. Anna Turner, Ravi Chavan, Niko Rodriguez, and Siena Moretti. Each had competed fiercely for a spot on the *Cloud Leopard.*

Each had lost.

"What, did you think you guys were the only ones up here?" Anna jeered. "Outer space is a big place. You never know who you'll run into."

"But—but—but—" Dash felt himself sputtering. Anna had that effect on him. She was always so sure she knew better than everyone else, especially Dash. And she loved rubbing it in his face. She was smart and tough and, most of the time, annoyingly right. Dash and the others had been sure she would be chosen for the mission.

They'd all been secretly relieved when she wasn't.

Well, maybe not so secretly.

Piper jumped in. "I think what Dash is trying to say is, how did you get here?" She said it nicely, even though Anna had been even ruder to her than she'd been to the rest of them. Piper always tried not to hold a grudge. Wasn't winning the best revenge?

"And what are you guys *doing* up here?" Piper added.

"Yeah, weird timing for a pleasure cruise," Gabriel said.

"In a multibillion-dollar ship," Carly added.

Anna peered over her glasses at the Alpha team. She and her crew were wearing uniforms of their own. They were all black, with an omega symbol emblazoned across the shoulder. "We're doing the same thing you're doing," Anna said, like it was the dumbest question ever. "Hunting down elements, trying to save the Earth—ring a bell?"

"I don't get it," Dash said.

Anna laughed. "Talk about the understatement of the century."

"Did Commander Phillips decide to send a second ship?" It certainly wouldn't be the first time Shawn Phillips had kept important information to himself. Dash turned to Chris, whose expression was grave. If there were another ship, Chris would know about it. But Chris looked as lost as the rest of them. Dash realized it was the first time he'd ever seen the older boy caught off balance.

"Commander Phillips?" Anna laughed, and the rest of

her crew joined in. "No, don't worry, your precious Phillips still thinks you four are his best bet. Lucky for Earth, we found someone who knows better."

"Who?" Dash said. He hated being out of the loop, having to beg Anna for answers. Anna was loving every second of it.

"If you must know, it was—" Anna stopped abruptly. Dash could hear a voice offscreen, but he wasn't able to make out the words. Anna's lips narrowed into a tight, straight line. Dash recognized that look: it was the face Anna made when someone told her what to do. "It's none of your business, that's who," she told Dash tersely. "What matters is that the *Omega* team is going to get all the elements long before you Alpha losers do."

"Nice to see you haven't changed, Anna," Carly said sarcastically.

Gabriel snorted. "Yeah, still totally delusional."

"She's simply being accurate," Siena said. Unlike the others, she didn't sound like she was boasting or rubbing it in their face. She was simply stating a fact. "Our odds of success are substantially higher than yours. For reasons we're not allowed to share."

"Look, we both care about finding the elements and getting back home," Dash said. He didn't like this situation any more than the others did, but he was the team leader. He had to think about what was best for the mission. Anna and the others were here now, and two ships had to be better than one, right? "Why don't we team up?"

Carly, Piper, and Gabriel looked at Dash in surprise. "Team up with them? You've got to be joking," Gabriel said.

Commander Phillips had chosen the Alphas partly because they were so good at teamwork. Niko, Ravi, Siena, and especially Anna, on the other hand, had proven they worked best alone.

"With two ships and two crews, we might be able to find the elements twice as fast," Dash pointed out.

"Team up? Forget it," Anna said. "We don't need you Alphas slowing us down."

"Maybe we should think about it," Siena said quietly. "Statistically our odds of success increase if—"

She abruptly cut herself off. Once again, there was the sound of someone talking offscreen. This time, the figure came over and joined the rest of the crew. He was a few years older than the others, with a pair of squarish black glasses perched on his stern face. "This is Colin, the fifth member of our crew," Anna said, sounding none too happy about it.

Dash thought it was only on TV that people's jaws dropped. But now his mouth popped wide open. Piper, Gabriel, and Carly wore identical expressions of cartoon shock. Four pairs of eyes turned to Chris. Then back to Colin. They swiveled back and forth, back and forth, like they were watching a tennis game.

Dash thought he must be imagining things. But no, it was real—except for the glasses, the boy on the *Light Blade* looked *exactly* like Chris.

Except that Dash had never seen Chris smile like Colin. Like he was watching a colony of ants scurry around beneath a magnifying glass. Like he was thinking very seriously about setting those ants on fire. Then stomping them.

"What is this?" Chris said. His voice was as expressionless as ever, but Dash had gotten to know him pretty well over the last few months. He could tell that the older boy was shaken. "How is this possible?"

"I think we've wasted enough time chatting," Colin snapped. Even his voice was exactly the same as Chris's. Except while Chris always sounded calm and friendly, Colin's words were coated with ice. "May the best team win. And trust me . . ." He stepped aside to reveal a large bone-white object sitting at the center of the navigation deck. It was the other piece of the Raptogon tooth, the piece they had left behind on planet J-16. "We will."

The screen went black.

"Wow," Piper said. She couldn't pull her gaze away from Chris. "That was . . . unexpected."

"That guy was definitely older than thirteen," Carly said. "How can he survive Gamma Speed? I thought Chris was the only one who could do that."

"*That's* what you think is weird about this?" Gabriel asked. "That he's a teenager? Did you see his *face*?" He was staring at Chris too. "What's the deal—do you have an identical twin or something?"

Chris shook his head. "Definitely not."

"Maybe a long-lost twin?" Carly suggested. "Separated at birth, like in a TV movie or something."

"Or maybe it was a clone," Gabriel said. "Anyone ever mention anything about cloning you, Chris?"

"There's no such thing as clones," Carly said.

"Oh yeah? Then what do you think's going on?" Gabriel countered.

"Maybe, uh . . . he's a robot," Carly suggested.

"A robot designed to look and talk exactly like Chris," Piper said, giggling at the idea.

"Only instead of cheeseburgers, he eats motor oil," Gabriel added.

"Okay, okay, so probably not a robot," Carly gave in. "What do you think, Dash?"

Dash was watching Chris carefully. The older boy wasn't giving anything away with his expression. "I think I want to know what Chris thinks."

"I think there's no point in speculating without any data," Chris said. He sounded perfectly calm, as usual. Like he hadn't just gotten the biggest surprise of his life. "Let's not get distracted by things that don't matter."

"There's another ship following us through space, and they've got their own *you,* and you don't think that matters?" Carly said in disbelief.

"Whoever he is, he's not me," Chris snapped. Something about the way he said it made Dash wonder if his feelings were hurt. But there was no way of telling from his face. "We're to launch our extraction mission to Meta Prime, where we'll find the second element. *That's* what matters right now."

"Uh, Chris is right," Dash said, because on the one hand, he was. On the other hand, Anna Turner was out there commanding her own ship with a duplicate copy of Chris on board. Which seemed more than a little relevant. "Let's meet in the docking bay in an hour for a mission briefing so we can get down to the surface ASAP."

Chris nodded sharply and left the room.

"So, that was weird," Gabriel said. "I mean, he's always weird, but that was special recipe weird, am I wrong?"

"No, that was definitely weird," Piper said. It was unusual for Chris to snap like that. Was he more concerned by the other ship and his impossible twin than he was willing to admit?

"We should make contact with Earth," Dash said. "Phillips will want to know about this."

"You're assuming he doesn't already," Gabriel pointed out.

Dash shook his head. "No way would he—"

"Keep life-altering secrets from us?" Gabriel cut in. "Fail to tell us the most important things about our own mission until it's too late for us to do anything about it? Send us into space without mentioning we might not make it home again?"

Dash couldn't argue with any of it.

But he still couldn't believe Commander Phillips would keep something like *this* from them. "Only one way to find out," he said.

Carly opened up a communications channel with Earth—or at least, she tried to.

"Nothing but static," she reported. Communications with home were patchy, especially once they left Gamma Speed. Sometimes it took days to get a clear signal.

"Are you freaking kidding me?" Gabriel snorted. "Most advanced piece of technology humanity's ever built, and it can't manage a stupid phone call."

"It's a 'stupid phone call' across several million light-years," Piper pointed out.

"We'll keep trying," Dash said, "but in the meantime, it looks like we're on our own with this."

"What else is new?" Gabriel grumbled. "It's not like he'd tell us anything, anyway."

"What now?" Carly said. "Should we go after Chris? Try to get him to tell us what's going on?"

"What makes you think he knows any more than we do?" Dash asked.

"Come on, he obviously knows *something*," Gabriel said. "Something more than he's telling us at least."

"If he does, he must have a good reason to keep it to

himself," Dash said diplomatically. They had agreed that if the five of them were going to work together as a crew, they would have to trust one another.

Carly frowned. She trusted Chris too—or at least, she was trying to. But Carly wasn't the type to trust *anyone* completely. "I really hope you're right about that."

Dash hoped so too.

Dash headed down the *Cloud Leopard*'s central corridor toward Chris's private quarters. That room had no connection to the ship's tubing system. There was only one way in: knocking.

Before he reached the door, Dash tried to step into one of the restricted passageways. He always did that when he was in this part of the ship.

And, as always, a force field bounced him gently away.

Commander Phillips had told them these restricted areas contained delicate equipment that they couldn't risk damaging, and that's why the crew was barred entrance.

They'd believed him, because they had no reason not to.

Then it had turned out that one of the restricted rooms contained *Chris*.

After that, Dash couldn't help wondering what else was hidden away behind closed doors. And he couldn't stop trying to get in, just in case, one of these times, the force field malfunctioned and let him pass.

Dash continued on to Chris's door and knocked. It slid open with a soft hiss.

"I told you, I know nothing about that . . . *person* on the other ship," Chris said, blocking the entrance. He still sounded pretty testy. "If you don't believe that, I'm sorry."

"I believe you," Dash said. "That's not why I'm here. It's time for, uh—but if this isn't a good time, I can—"

"Oh, no, of course," Chris said, stepping out of the doorway. "In all the commotion, I had forgotten your injections."

Dash was taken aback. He'd never known Chris to forget anything. Especially anything this important.

Chris was the only one who knew his secret, that he was six months older than the others—which was six months older than he was supposed to be. Dash would turn fourteen by the time their mission ended. And anyone older than fourteen might not survive traveling in Gamma Speed. Chris, the super-genius, had apparently designed some kind of serum for himself that would protect him from Gamma effects. But all Dash had was an experimental daily injection that was supposed to slow down his metabolism. There was no guarantee it would work—or for how long. If they didn't get back to Earth on schedule . . .

Dash shook it off. It was important not to think about

that. He'd taken a risk coming on this mission, he knew that. But saving the Earth—saving his mom and Abby? That was worth it. Still, he didn't want the others knowing he was taking such a risk; he didn't want them to worry. Dash shared a room with Gabriel, which didn't offer much privacy. So Chris had agreed he could move his store of injectors here, to make sure his secret didn't get out.

"It's okay," Dash said, stepping inside. "It's no big deal."

"It is the biggest of deals," Chris pointed out. "If you don't receive your injection every twenty-four hours, the consequences will be dire. And potentially fatal."

"Uh, yeah, thanks," Dash said. "I try not to think about that. I just meant, it's no big deal you forgot. There's a lot going on."

"This is, as your friend Anna might say, the understatement of the century." Chris smiled.

"Chris, dude, did you just make a joke?"

Chris was a nice guy, a brilliant guy, but he was more than a little lacking in the sense of humor category.

"I made an effort," Chris admitted.

"Not bad," Dash said. "We'll work on it."

Chris's quarters were pretty much the most personality-free bedroom Dash had ever seen. In Dash and Gabriel's bunk, Gabriel had tacked up posters of antique aircraft all over his wall. Dash covered his with a gigantic star chart. Photos of their families were scattered across every remaining surface. Dash hadn't seen the girls' room, but he was sure they were pretty much the same. Except maybe with more pink.

Chris's quarters, on the other hand, were bare. Not empty: the space was crowded with high-tech equipment, screens, controls—it was almost like a second bridge, and Dash suspected that if Chris wanted to, he could fly the ship from here. But who wanted to *live* on a flight deck? Chris hadn't done anything to make the space his own. There were no posters, no pictures, no reminders of where he'd come from or the people he left behind, nothing.

Dash sat down at the bare desk and pulled one of the disposable injectors out of the case. It was an experimental biologic, designed to halt cellular growth. Supposedly, it was freezing Dash's body at exactly the age it was now so he wouldn't get old enough that Gamma Speed would kill him.

Supposedly.

It hadn't been tested on anyone. Until now.

Dash held his breath and jammed the injector into his thigh. It was like an EpiPen—all you had to do was aim it and press a button. There was a quick stab of pain, no sharper than if he'd jabbed himself hard with a pencil.

Dash was glad it didn't hurt more, but he still hated this part of his day more than any other.

It was the one time he couldn't force himself to forget about the ticking clock.

Rocket, Chris's golden retriever, padded over and knelt by Dash's side. Dash ruffled his soft hair and let the dog nuzzle his hand, wondering if Rocket had any idea how far he was from home.

"So where do you really think that ship came from?" he asked Chris, trying to distract himself.

"As I have told you, I do not know—"

"Yeah, I got that. But, I mean, if you had to make a bet, where would you put your money?"

"Well . . . I think the ship came from Earth," Chris said slowly.

"Yeah, the crew kind of gave that away. But who could have sent it?"

"This betting that you want me to do, it's an activity for those without enough facts to make an informed decision, is it not?"

The only betting Dash ever did involved betting quarters in lunchtime poker games. "I guess you could say that."

"I am a person who prefers facts," Chris said. "I'll hold on to my money until I have more."

"Anyone ever tell you you're kind of a strange guy?" Dash said, smiling.

"Many people. But perhaps they are the strange ones."

"Uh, yeah," Dash allowed. "Perhaps."

❋　　❋　　❋

Orbit.

The ship spiraled around Meta Prime, trapped by its puny gravitational field. Miles and miles beneath them lay the second stop on their impossible mission. The *Cloud Cat* gleamed beside the docking bay doors, ready to carry an extraction team down to the planet.

While in Gamma Speed, the crew had devoured every known fact about Meta Prime. There weren't many. It was a dwarf planet encrusted with machinery—but, according to the unmanned probes that had flown over years before, no signs of life. Meta Prime had a liquid metal core, fueled by a substance called Magnus 7.

That's what they were after. The second element. The thing that would bring them one step closer to getting the Source and getting home. The ship only had enough power for an outbound trip. If they ever wanted to make it back, they needed to acquire extracts of all six elements.

Even a single failure would doom the mission.

Which meant right now, there was nothing more important than getting down to the planet, and getting it right.

"Preliminary readings confirm no signs of organic life," Carly said once the crew had gathered in the docking bay. She'd spent the last hour monitoring the planet from her lab workstation, processing all the data she could. Carly believed in information, in facts. If you had enough of them, she thought, you could understand the whole universe. "It looks like the old scans we have are still accurate. There's definitely a lot of machinery down on the surface, but it's not putting out much of an electro-magnetic signal. Whatever was down there isn't working anymore."

"If there is machinery on the planet, then someone built it," Chris reminded them. "Intelligent life was present here once."

"Couldn't have been too intelligent, or they'd still be around," Gabriel pointed out.

"Still, I suggest you proceed with caution."

"We?" Dash said. "I take it that means you haven't changed your mind about coming down to the surface with us?"

"As I've explained, my extensive knowledge about the ship and the mission is too valuable to risk on—"

"Yeah, yeah, we know, you and your big brain have to stay up here where it's safe," Gabriel said. "Leave the rest of us to do the dirty work."

Chris ignored the sarcasm. Or maybe he didn't hear it. "Precisely. I'll stay on the ship monitoring your com-munications. There's significant electrical interference in the atmosphere, so maintaining contact when you're on the surface might prove difficult. You could end up on your own," Chris warned.

"We can handle that," Dash said.

Chris nodded. "I know you can."

Dash suppressed a smile.

"You'll need to retrieve a sample of Magnus 7," Chris reminded them. "There's a river of molten lava cutting through the center of the landing site—you'll extract the Magnus 7 from that."

"Yeah, we know," Gabriel said, ducking a cloud of ZRKs. The small robots buzzed around the *Cloud Cat*, readying the shuttle for the journey. "What we don't know is how we're supposed to get it back up to the ship. We can't exactly bring molten lava home in our pockets."

"No, not at seven thousand degrees Fahrenheit you can't," Chris agreed, almost cheerfully.

There was nothing on the ship with the capacity to hold that kind of material. They would have to find some sort of container on the planet.

"I believe you will not be disappointed by what you find," Chris added. "If the intelligence that designed this machinery is as sophisticated as it seems, I'm sure it will have left something useful behind."

"I thought you didn't like to make guesses without all the facts," Dash said, assembling his gear for the mission.

Chris had a funny look on his face, like a cat that had gotten away with something. "In this case, I have all the facts I need."

"So, Chris and Piper will stay up on the ship," Dash said. Even though they were pretty sure the machinery on the planet was dead and abandoned, there was a chance they were wrong. And back at Base Ten, they'd seen what

the Meta Prime machines could do in action. The Alphas had finally beat them by shutting off the power that fed the simulation.

It was Carly who'd realized that maybe they could do the same thing on the real Meta Prime. The *Cloud Leopard* could send out a targeted electromagnetic pulse that would shut down all electrical activity in the immediate area. There was no guarantee it would work, and Dash was hoping they'd never have to find out. Still, Carly had spent several days drilling Piper on everything she needed to know about EMPs. Just in case.

"You all set, Piper?"

Piper grinned. "Aye, aye, Captain."

"Uh, actually, Dash, I've been thinking we should make a little change in plans," Carly said quickly. "I'm going to stay up on the ship. Piper can go down to the surface."

"You're bringing this up *now*?" he said.

Carly gave him a sheepish smile. "Better now than once we're already halfway down to the surface?"

Dash couldn't believe it. Didn't they have enough to worry about without a last-minute substitution? Besides, Carly had stayed up on the ship for their last planetary expedition. It didn't make any sense she would volunteer to do it again. "What's going on, Carly? What's this about?"

"This ship is my job, Dash. I know it inside and out.

You know that. If anything unexpected happens down there and you need backup from the *Cloud Leopard*, I want to be there to be sure you get it."

"You don't think I can handle it?" Piper said, looking hurt.

"No, that's not it," Carly said quickly. "I just . . . I think I can serve this mission better if I stay on board the *Cloud Leopard*. I know I can."

"I don't like it," Dash said. "We planned all this out ahead of time for a reason. You make changes at the last minute, you get sloppy."

Carly glared at him, her temper flaring. "Fine. Whatever. Feel free to ignore what I think. You're in charge, right?"

"Come on, Dash," Gabriel said. "It's no big deal who stays and who goes. And you know Carly knows this ship better than anyone."

Carly shot him a grateful look.

"Other than me, of course," Gabriel added.

Dash turned to Piper, uncertain. "What do you think, Piper? Are you okay with joining the extraction team?"

"Whatever you think is best, Dash," she said.

Gabriel and Carly shared an eye roll. Dash pretended not to see. He hadn't known how tough it was to be a leader, especially when it meant leading his friends. Sometimes—like when they bickered over who got the last slice of pizza—they were like any other friends. All on the same level, messing around about stupid stuff, entertaining themselves with arguments where it didn't matter who won.

When they went into mission mode, it was like flipping a switch. Suddenly, Dash wasn't one of them anymore—he was, sort of, the *boss* of them.

Being in charge made the whole friendship thing tricky sometimes.

And being friends sometimes made the in-charge thing seem impossible.

Times like now.

"Okay," he said. It went against his every instinct, but instincts could be wrong. "Carly stays up here with Chris. Everyone else, prepare for departure."

Chris headed up to the bridge, from where he would monitor the *Cloud Cat*'s journey. Piper raced back to her quarters to change into something more mission-ready, and Dash checked over the ZRKs' work on the shuttle. He wanted to make triple-sure it was good to go.

Gabriel lingered for a moment. "You sure about this?" he asked Carly quietly. "Aren't you getting a little sick of being stuck in this tin can? Don't you want to breathe some fresh alien air?"

"It doesn't matter what I want," she told him. "This is for the good of the mission."

He gave her a skeptical look. Then, serious for once, he said, "You know, if there's something else, you can always tell me."

She pressed her lips together and gave him a light punch on the arm. "Good luck down there. Don't get blown up by any robots."

Gabriel winked. "Hey, you know me, I've got metal in my veins. I'm practically part machine. They'll recognize me as one of their own."

Carly smiled—and she managed to keep that smile frozen on her face until she was safely out of the docking bay and on her own.

Then it disappeared.

Finally alone, Carly sagged against the corridor wall, fighting back tears. What had she just done? Had she screwed up the mission for her own stupid, selfish reasons?

She let Dash believe she'd been thinking about it for a while, but that was a lie.

It wasn't until she stepped into the docking bay and her knees nearly buckled beneath her that she knew she couldn't go down to the planet. She had to stay on the *Cloud Leopard.* Not because she thought she knew more than Piper. Or because she thought it would help the mission.

She wanted to stay on the ship because she was afraid of leaving it.

She, Carly Diamond, youngest member of the crew and determined to be the toughest, was afraid.

She knew this ship. She'd spent six months studying the *Cloud Leopard* back on Earth, memorizing every inch of it. Nothing up here could surprise her. But an alien planet? That was another story. Anything could happen down there. *Anything.* There was nothing Carly hated more than being scared—and nothing that scared her more than the unknown.

She told herself she wasn't letting down the crew or the mission, and that the others would never know the truth. But *she* knew. And that was almost worse.

The *Cloud Cat* streaked toward the atmosphere, carving a line of fire through the sky. Inside the small ship, Dash, Gabriel, and Piper were strapped into their flight seats, watching the planet loom in the window. Swirling red-and-brown clouds blanketed the surface, making it impossible to see what lay beneath. The atmosphere churned and sparked with electrical storms.

It was going to be a rough ride.

Gabriel peered through his dark flight glasses, his palm resting on a smooth plate that could pick up every twitch of a finger. He steered the shuttle steadily as they dropped out of orbit, preparing for a rocky atmospheric entry. The computer had plotted out a course based on the old scans from the unmanned probe. But those scans were years out of date. Conditions on the ground might have changed since then, and the computer would have no way of knowing.

It was a lesson they'd learned on J-16—a lesson they'd almost learned too late.

"Fasten your seat belts," Gabriel told Dash and Piper. "It's about to be an extremely bumpy ride."

Dash gripped the edges of his seat. "Just be careful—"

The last word flew out of his mouth as Gabriel pushed the throttle into high gear. They plunged beneath the clouds and plummeted toward the surface of the planet.

The flight glasses allowed Gabriel to control the ship with the tiniest of eye movements. It felt like his mind fused with the engine. Like the ship was an extension of his body. They sliced through the air at hundreds of miles an hour. Every millisecond counted. But Gabriel was totally relaxed. You couldn't fly tense. You had to give in to the motion, become one with the speed.

40

He pushed the shuttle faster, and faster still.

He was in total control.

No matter how it felt to his passengers.

Piper sat quietly, her eyes closed, trying not to puke. She kept a thin smile fixed on her face, just in case Dash and Gabriel were paying attention. (They weren't.)

Dash fiddled with his backup glasses, willing himself to trust Gabriel. They weren't going to crash.

They weren't going to slam into a wall of machinery or spin out of control.

They weren't going to smash into the ground at full speed and explode on impact.

Gabriel wouldn't let those things happen. Dash knew that. Just like he knew Gabriel was the better pilot, by far.

Still, he wished he were flying the ship himself.

They closed in on their landing site. Gabriel took it low and fast, skimming over and around rusted machinery. Two enormous, flat gray structures stretched for miles across the planet's surface. A thin red ribbon of fire sliced between them. That was the river of lava, where they would find the element. They hoped.

The shuttle banked hard to the right, then dove sharply, its nose pointed at the ground.

"Pull up!" Dash yelped. It looked like they were headed straight into the river of fire.

"Easy," Gabriel murmured. "Give it a minute."

"In a minute we'll be swimming in molten lava," Dash insisted. "Pull up!"

"I got this," Gabriel said.

The *Cloud Cat* plummeted down and down. Piper's stomach was turning somersaults. Dash was about to seize control when, at the very last second, they pulled out of the dive.

The *Cloud Cat* veered up, skimming along the river. Fire lapped at their belly. Huge metal walls rose on either side of them, scraping the clouds. The *Cloud Cat* sped through the narrow alley, tracing the river, weaving back and forth, hugging its curves. Until . . .

"Brace yourselves," Gabriel warned. "Touchdown in three . . ."

Dash held on tight.

Piper held her breath.

"Two . . ."

The *Cloud Cat* banked shallowly to the left, aiming for a narrow bare spot along the bank. It was barely as wide as the ship.

"One . . ."

There was no room for miscalculation. Too far to the left and they'd crash into the wall. Too far to the right and they'd be neck-deep in lava.

"Touchdown!" Gabriel shouted as the *Cloud Cat* settled into the dirt with a bone-rattling thud.

Piper let out her breath in a huge whoosh of relief. Dash thumped Gabriel on the back. "You got it, man!"

"You sound surprised," Gabriel said.

Dash laughed. "How should I sound?"

"*Awed* is always welcome," Gabriel suggested. "I'll also accept *amazed, intimidated,* or *blown away.*"

"Can we settle on the right adjective later?" Piper said. "We've got an element to retrieve." The sooner they got started, the sooner they could get safely back to the ship.

Hopefully.

Dash and the others stepped cautiously out onto the surface. Dash took a deep breath. It amazed him that there were alien planets with atmospheres just like Earth's. According to their scans, the air here had exactly the same proportions of oxygen and nitrogen. But it tasted different: almost metallic, like the taste of biting your lip and drawing blood.

They stood on the banks of a gushing river. It ran

red with molten lava, bubbles of fire popping and fizzing against the shore. The ground was charred black, scored with cracks and fissures where the lava had bored through. Alongside each bank, the sheer wall of machinery rose up—and up and up and up until it disappeared into the thick red clouds. It felt like they were standing at the bottom of a narrow, impossibly steep canyon.

"So this is Meta Prime," Gabriel said in a hushed voice. "Wow." Aside from the rushing river, the planet was absolutely still. No signs of life except for the three of them. But for some reason, Gabriel still felt like he should whisper.

Like someone was listening.

"Yeah," Dash said quietly. The stillness of this place, the emptiness, was a little creepy. Like one of those fairytale towns where everyone had fallen under a spell and slept for a century. He didn't want to be the one to wake them. "Wow."

"At least there are no Raptogons here," Piper said. "Definitely my favorite planet so far."

"Out of two," Gabriel said drily.

She steered her air chair toward a cluster of small alien robots that were frozen in place on the riverbank. They were boxy little creatures, with bodies like trapezoids balanced on two stubby feet.

Piper gave one of the little robots a gentle tap.

"Piper!" Dash hissed. "What are you doing?"

"I just wanted to see if it would wake up," she said.

"Why would we want it to wake up?" Dash asked in alarm. After their adventure on J-16, he'd been looking forward to a planet without any signs of life. No aliens meant nothing that could eat them.

"I think it's dead," Piper said a little sadly. "Or inert, or whatever you call it when it's a machine. It can't hurt us." The little robots were everywhere, frozen dots on the dead landscape. "It's like all the people just up and left," she said in wonder. "But why would they leave these little guys behind?"

"Maybe they didn't have a choice," Dash said. He was starting to get a bad feeling about this place. The whole planet felt like it was holding its breath, waiting for something to happen. "Maybe they left in a hurry."

"There's a lot of damage on these walls," Gabriel said, pointing at the torn and twisted metal. "And those rusty things sticking out kind of look like cannons. Hey, you think there was some kind of battle here?"

"I'm afraid there's about to be," Piper said, only half joking, as the clouds split open and a blazing light streaked toward them.

"I really hope that's not what I think it is," Gabriel said. But it was: a shuttle, coming in for a landing on the patch of ground directly across the river from them.

Dash clapped his hands over his ears to block out the deafening roar of its engines. As the ship touched down, Gabriel spotted Anna at the controls. He thought the

44

pointy shuttle looked like a praying mantis—or maybe a cockroach—but it still deserved a better pilot.

The engines shut down, and Anna, Siena, and Niko climbed out.

"What do you think you're doing here?" Gabriel called out. "Or do you just get a kick out of following us around?"

"We're doing the same thing you are," Anna shouted back. "Just faster. And better. As usual."

"You wish!"

Anna laughed. "You Alphas have no idea what's going on down here, do you?" she shouted.

The two crews faced off at the narrowest point of the river, a few yards apart but just close enough to hear one another over the rushing lava. No one wanted to get too close to the bank and risk getting a gush of molten fire in the face.

"We know as much as you do," Dash called back.

The Omega team laughed. "So Chris told you everything?" Anna asked. *"Everything?"*

"What's she getting at?" Piper asked quietly. "And how does she know about Chris?"

Dash and Gabriel shrugged. You never knew what Anna was trying to do—except win.

"Of course he did!" Dash shouted, trying to sound more confident than he felt.

This wasn't Base Ten; they weren't fighting for a spot

on the mission. That competition was over, and Dash had won. Anna may have forgotten that, but he hadn't.

"So you know about the sloggers?" Niko asked. "And about the war?"

"Uh, war?" Gabriel murmured.

That did *not* sound good.

"What war?" Dash called.

As he spoke, an ear-shattering scream of metal on metal sliced through the air. The ground shook.

"Uh-oh," Gabriel said.

"What's going on?" Piper cried as, all around them, machinery groaned and creaked back to life.

"I'm gonna guess nothing good," Gabriel said.

"Look," Dash said, fear almost swallowing the word. "Look at the robots."

The strange little machines along the riverbank were frozen no longer.

They marched in lockstep toward the river, scooping molten fire into their metal bellies, then clomping back toward the wall of machinery. A gray door slid open and, one by one, swallowed them into darkness. Up and down the walls, rusted cannons swiveled slowly toward the opposing bank.

"*That* war!" Anna shouted, fleeing for cover as one of the cannons on the Alphas' side of the river shot a flaming ball of lava into the air.

Suddenly, the air was filled with fire.

"Run!" Dash cried.

Gabriel, Dash, and Piper fled down the riverbank as fast as they could, searching desperately for cover. Heat seared their skin. Fireballs whizzed overhead, exploding on impact. Twisted shards of metal rained from the sky.

"Over here!" Dash spotted a crevice in the wall. It was only about two feet deep, but it would give them a chance to figure out their next move.

"Chris didn't mention he was dumping us in the middle of a *war*," Gabriel complained, gasping for air.

"How was he supposed to know?" Dash said.

"Well, the Omegas sure knew," Gabriel pointed out. "Who told *them*?"

"Guys, it doesn't matter who knew what," Piper said. "The question is what do we do now? How are we supposed to get to the element in the middle of *that*?"

Dash knew Piper was right. That was the important question.

He just didn't have an answer.

"Chris? Carly?" he said into the Mobile Tech Band strapped around his wrist. It connected him to the ship's massive database of knowledge—and, just as important, the rest of his crew. "You guys have any ideas from up there?"

He expected to see Carly's face peering back at him from the small MTB screen, but there was nothing. Only static.

He tried again. "Hello? *Cloud Leopard*? Do you read me?"

"It must be the atmosphere," Piper said. "Chris warned us about that."

"Or electromagnetic interference," Gabriel suggested. "If this whole planet just came back online, it must be putting out a truckload of EM waves."

It didn't matter why they'd lost the signal.

One way or another, it was gone. There was no way to contact the *Cloud Leopard*.

They were on their own.

"**What do you** mean we lost the signal?" Carly shouted. She whacked the monitor, as if she could jar it back to life. A flock of ZRKs squealed in alarm and flitted into the air, hovering around her like they were just waiting for her to break something.

And it didn't even help: there was still nothing but static.

"This is not a broken vending machine," Chris warned her. "Please be careful."

"Be careful? I'm not the one on an alien planet without any backup! I'm not the one who has to worry about being careful!"

"Please stay calm," Chris said.

"How am I supposed to stay calm? We have no idea what's happening down there, no way of helping them or knowing what's happening to them." Carly slammed her hand against the side of her flight seat in frustration.

That hurt.

She took a deep breath, then another. "Okay, I'm calm." It wasn't true, but maybe after a few more deep breaths it would be.

Carly was furious with the ship, with the atmospheric interference, with Chris for being so calm, and with the crew for being so far away, but mostly she was furious with herself. She'd been too big a wimp to go down to the planet, and now she was up here safe and sound while her friends could be facing anything. And she couldn't even help them. She couldn't even *talk* to them. She was supposed to know the ship well enough to handle any crisis that came up.

But she couldn't even manage a stupid radio signal.

"We knew this might happen," Chris reminded her. "The atmosphere is filled with electrical storms. Communication will be difficult."

"There's really nothing we can do?" Carly asked.

"Nothing but wait."

She'd never been good at waiting. If Dash and the others were cut off, it seemed like she should be *doing* something about it.

"Why don't you go down to the library," Chris suggested, as if he knew exactly what she was thinking. "Maybe you can find something in the records about boosting our signal strength."

"You don't think I should stay here with you? In case the signal comes back?"

"I'll keep monitoring the line," Chris assured her. "I'll

let you know as soon as anything changes. If the storms clear, we should be able to get through."

"And what about in the meantime?" Carly said. "What if something happens down there and they can't reach us? What if they need our help?" She didn't understand how Chris could be so calm about this.

"Everything is going to be fine," Chris said. "I'm sure of it."

Carly frowned. "That makes one of us."

"Come in, *Cloud* Leopard." Dash, Gabriel, and Piper had pressed themselves against the towering wall, beneath a shallow overhang that shielded them from the rain of fire. They were safe . . . for now. But they were also trapped. They couldn't find any way inside the complex—there were no doors, just a towering wall that stretched infinitely long and high. If they couldn't get inside, they couldn't hunt for something strong enough to contain the Magnus 7.

Not to mention, they'd apparently landed in the middle of a war.

It was exactly the kind of terrible, horrible, no good, very bad situation they'd prepared an emergency backup plan for. Unfortunately, the plan required the *Cloud Leopard*.

And the *Cloud Leopard* wasn't responding.

"*Cloud Leopard*, this is Dash." Maybe even though he couldn't hear them, they could hear him. "We're pinned down on the surface of the planet by some kind of battle. Not sure how we're going to secure the element, but . . ." Dash tried to sound sure of himself. Like a leader would. "We'll find a way. So if you can hear us up there—"

"WHO IS THIS?"

The voice boomed in their earpieces.

It wasn't Chris. It wasn't Carly.

It was a deep, ancient-sounding voice, and it wasn't happy.

"Who are you to trespass on my world?" the voice said.

Dash, Piper, and Gabriel exchanged a terrified glance. Dash cleared his throat. "Who are *you*?" he said.

There was a pause, as if the voice was considering how to repay his rudeness. And then: "I am Lord Garquin, and this is my world. Give me one reason why I shouldn't wipe you off the face of it."

6

"**Well?**" **the voice** boomed. "I'm *waiting*. Explain yourselves, or bear the consequences."

Dash wondered if it was possible for his heart to thump itself right out of his chest.

"It's an alien," Piper whispered, her eyes wide with wonder.

"No kidding," Gabriel said, trying to sound cool. He wasn't doing a very good job.

They'd seen a lot of amazing things since joining the Alpha mission. Ships that could fly across the universe, robots that could speak (and quote bad movies), air chairs, and Mobile Tech Bands and air tubes and ZRKs. Not to mention the ten-times-more-terrifying-than-a-T.-rex Raptogon they'd faced down on J-16. They'd had their minds blown again and again. But none of it came close to this.

Alien intelligence.

A real live alien talking into their ears.

It didn't make any sense. The scans had shown no

signs of life—so who was this voice that sounded like a bad guy from a video game, talking to them on their private communication channel, talking in *English,* of all things?

"Do you think it could be a machine?" Dash asked. "A robot? Or a recording?"

The voice cleared its throat, a deep, terrifying rumble. "Am I to assume you choose *bear the consequences*?"

"Uh, I don't think that's a recording," Gabriel said. "Maybe you should answer the guy."

"Quickly," Piper added. She could see that Dash was worried about saying the wrong thing. "It's okay."

He figured he had two options. He could make up an answer he thought this Lord Garquin would like and pray it didn't get them blown off the face of the planet.

Or he could tell the truth.

Dash took a deep breath, hoping he was making the right choice. He brought his MTB closer to his mouth so the words would come through loud and clear. "We're from Earth, which is about a billion and a half miles from here. We're trying to save our planet. There's an element on your planet, Magnus 7. We just need a little of it, and then we'll take it back to our ship and you'll never see us again."

"You were planning to *steal* from me?" Lord Garquin shouted.

"Er . . . borrow?"

"You were going to give it *back*?" Lord Garquin said.

"Well . . ." Dash looked wildly at Gabriel and Piper, but they had no ideas either. "No. I guess we weren't."

"So you're thieves. Here to steal from me and my world."

There was a long, terrifying pause.

Then Lord Garquin chuckled. The sound was warm and reassuring in their ears. "I respect your honesty."

Dash let out all his breath at once. Scary alien overlords didn't usually chuckle before blowing you up. At least, he didn't think they did.

He said, "So you don't mind if we just grab a little bit of Magnus 7 and get out of here."

"I didn't say that!" Lord Garquin boomed.

Dash looked at the others. *Worth a try,* he mouthed.

"But . . ." Garquin's voice trailed off.

They all perked up. *But* sounded promising.

"But what?" Piper asked. She was as nervous as the others about this mysterious voice in their ears—but she was also incredibly curious. Who *was* this guy? What did he want from them? How was he connected to the two walls of machines and the fireballs flying back and forth between them?

"But *perhaps* we can help each other," Lord Garquin said. "I just might know how you can collect some of this Magnus 7 you speak of—and *you* can help me win my war."

"I thought you said this was 'your world,'" Gabriel

said. "If the whole world belongs to you, then who are you at war with?"

"I may not have spoken with, er, absolute accuracy," Lord Garquin admitted. "This is my world, yes. But it is also Lord Cain's world. The two of us have divided it down the middle. On one side of the river lies my domain, a gleaming and beautiful kingdom of metallic wonders. On the other side of the river, my eternal opponent rules over his dark and decrepit land. He lurks behind his rusting and broken-down wall of cheap gadgetry, living only to torment me. You can, of course, tell from a glance which kingdom is which."

"Uh . . ." To Dash, the two towering walls seemed identically gray and featureless. "Sure. Of course you can."

Gabriel slapped a hand over his mouth, holding back a snicker.

Piper glared at both of them. "What happened between the two of you?" she asked Lord Garquin. "Why are you at war?"

"Why? Because . . . well, because we are," he said.

"I mean, what are you fighting for?" Piper clarified.

"We're fighting to win," said Lord Garquin. "What else is there?"

"Yeah, what else?" Gabriel agreed. Dash nodded.

Piper sighed and shook her head. *Boys.* Even the extraterrestrial ones were fixated on winning. On the other hand, if Carly were here, she probably would have been the first to agree. And Anna was the most uber-competitive person she'd ever met. Was Piper the only one who thought winning wasn't enough? That fighting should be *for* something?

Apparently.

"Our war stretches back through the ages," Lord Garquin continued. "But for many years now, we have lived in peace under a truce. Today, Lord Cain broke that truce. So as you can see, *I* am the injured party here."

"Injured party? Did you get hurt in the fighting?" Dash asked.

"And are you having a party to make yourself feel better?" Gabriel added.

"Injured party means that I'm the one who did no wrong," Lord Garquin said irritably. "Lord Cain attacked me with no warning, for no reason."

"Wait a second," Dash said, suddenly realizing what that meant. "The first shot came from *our* side of the river—do you mean we're in Lord Cain's territory?"

"Of course!" Lord Garquin said. "Can't you tell by the foul decrepitude?"

"Oh, right," Dash said quickly. He was getting nervous again. Whoever this Lord Cain was, surely he wouldn't like a bunch of strangers plotting with Lord Garquin on his turf.

"Lucky for us," Lord Garquin added, "there's something we *both* need over in Lord Cain's domain. So shall we help each other?"

"I don't know about this," Dash said. He was hesitant to get involved in some alien war. Especially when they didn't even know what the war was about.

"What if I told you that you had no other choice?" Lord Garquin said.

Dash didn't like the sound of that. It sounded a lot like blackmail. "How's that?"

"You've seen the little robots who collect lava from the river and bring it behind the wall?" Garquin said. "Those are the sloggers. Cain and I use them to collect the molten lava that powers our domains—but *you* could use one to carry the Magnus 7 safely back to your ship. That is, if I help you reprogram one to do it."

"And what do we have to do in return?" Dash asked.

"One of my sloggers is spying behind enemy lines. You should find it at the communications hub of Lord Cain's kingdom. When you find TULIP—"

"TULIP?" Gabriel echoed.

"The spy slogger."

"You named him TULIP?" Gabriel asked incredulously.

"I named *her* TULIP. Is there something wrong with that?"

"No," Dash said quickly, giving Gabriel a look that said *stop talking now.* "No, there definitely isn't."

"I thought not. So, when you find TULIP, she will guide you to the switch that governs Cain's control over his entire complex. You will flip off the switch and leave him powerless. Then, and only then, I will help you reprogram TULIP to collect and store the Magnus 7 you need. You see? It's very simple, and we both win."

"What I see is that we take all the risk, and win your war for you," Dash said, "while you stay nice and safe locked up behind your big, strong wall."

"Well, yes, that's another way of looking at it," Garquin said. "But my way is so much more pleasant, don't you think? Plus, there's this: if you agree to help, I will agree not to launch any fireballs at your side of the river until you get safely behind the wall."

"And if we don't agree?" Dash asked.

Lord Garquin burst into cheery laughter. "Who would be that foolish?" He chuckled. "Unless being incinerated sounds like your idea of fun?"

"He's right," Piper said in a low voice. "We don't have a choice."

"I know," Dash said, muting the radios for a moment. "I just don't like it." He was a little awed by the fact that he'd just been talking to an alien intelligence.

A little awed and more than a little freaked out.

"How do we know we can trust anything about this guy?" Dash said. "How do we know anything he's saying is true? There are a lot of things that don't add up."

"Like what?" Piper asked.

"Like how come he speaks English," Dash pointed out.

"He's a super-intelligent extraterrestrial," Gabriel said. "They always speak English. Or, for all we know, he's speaking Garquinese, and he's got some kind of super-advanced microscopic autotranslation device that turns whatever he says into something we can understand. That's how these things work."

"In the *movies*," Dash said. Sometimes he wondered if Gabriel thought he was starring in a movie of his very own. It was true that in the movies, the aliens almost always found a way to speak English. And it was usually pretty obvious who was a good guy and who was a bad guy. It was easy to know who to trust.

But this was real life.

Nothing was easy.

"Come on, don't you want to see what's behind the wall?" Gabriel asked. He was itching to get a look into all the machinery.

"I'm pretty sure this Lord Cain guy's behind the wall," Dash said. "And it doesn't sound like it'll be much fun if *he* sees *us.*"

"We'll be quick and quiet," Gabriel said. "You know we can do this. Not to mention we have to do it."

Dash wished that he could check in with Chris and Carly, but in the end, it didn't matter. There was no way around it—they needed the Magnus 7, and helping Lord Garquin was their best chance of getting it. "So we're all agreed?" he asked his team. This was a big decision. He didn't want to do it unless all three of them were on board.

"Like I said, we've got no other choice," Piper said.

"Let's win us a war," Gabriel said.

Dash switched the radio back on. "Okay," he told Lord Garquin. "Tell us what we need to do."

Chris watched Meta Prime through the view screen, trying to calm his nerves. From this distance, the planet looked like an unbroken sphere of gray. It looked whole and at peace. Chris knew better. This was a world rife with conflict. This was a world of machinery and destruction. A world torn between two masters who would stop at nothing to conquer all.

This was the world he had sent his crew off to. Dash, Piper, and Gabriel were down there, doing their best to survive. And they probably thought Chris had abandoned them.

Chris sighed. He'd thought he knew what he was getting them into. But something was wrong down on the planet's surface, something he couldn't explain. Something, perhaps, that had to do with the other spaceship matching their orbit. Or with the boy on that ship, the one who looked exactly like Chris.

Chris wondered if he should have told his crew the truth after all.

He hated lying to them, even if it was for their own good.

When they make it back to the ship, he promised himself, *I'll tell them everything.*

As soon as they made it back.

If they made it back.

Lord Garquin was as good as his word. At his direction, they shadowed the sloggers marching back and forth between the wall and the river. Piper, Dash, and Gabriel each fell into step beside one of the sloggers and marched toward the towering metal wall. A silver door slid open and shut, admitting one slogger at a time.

"You sure about this?" Dash murmured as he and his slogger drew closer to the door. It whooshed shut with great force and looked sharp enough to slice him in half.

The slogger itself didn't seem to know he was there. But Dash couldn't help but notice the small, raised circle at the center of its chest. It looked a lot like the muzzle of a gun.

This was exactly what he'd feared: the Base Ten training exercise come to life. *Those* sloggers had shot laser beams from their chests.

Those sloggers had also been holograms; their laser beams were harmless.

This time the Alpha team wouldn't be so lucky.

"Step through at the same time as the slogger and you'll be fine," Lord Garquin said.

There was no reason to trust the alien . . . but what else could he do? Dash glanced over his shoulder. Piper's air chair hovered alongside her slogger, and Gabriel and his slogger were bringing up the rear.

"Ready, guys? Here goes nothing." Dash and his slogger were up. The slogger stood before the immense wall, unleashing a series of beeps and chirps. The silver doorway slid up, and the slogger marched inside. Dash slipped through with him, just as the door slammed down. As it whooshed shut, he felt the hot rush of air at the back of his neck and shivered. It had been that close.

The door opened twice more, and Piper and Gabriel rejoined him. The three members of Team Alpha gazed around them in awe. Base Ten's holographic simulation of this place didn't begin to compare to the real thing.

It was a factory—a factory the size of a city, teeming with metal life. Conveyer belts crisscrossed through the air, swooping highways carrying sloggers wherever they needed to go. They stretched up and down as far as the eye could see. A column of flame shot up through the center of the vast space, held in place by what must have been some kind of force field. Metal tubes transported flaming lava back toward the outer wall, funneling it into giant cannons. Tunnels and corridors wrapped snakelike around the column of fire, spiraling up and up. There must have been miles of them.

Everything was in motion, not just the sloggers and the conveyer belts, but the walls themselves. Every surface was covered by steel and brass machinery, dials and readouts, flickering needles and flashing displays, clomping pistons and spinning gears.

Gabriel felt like he had seen this place in his dreams. A land of machines, everything governed by rules. By specific, understandable physical laws. A world where you could take anything and everything apart to see how it worked. This was the way a world *should* be, Gabriel thought. It was the strangest place he'd ever been, and he had never felt more at home.

Dash, on the other hand, had seen this moving checkerboard floor in his nightmares. There was no solid ground between them and the corridors wrapping around the central column. Instead, the air whizzed with flying brass plates that deposited sloggers from one conveyer belt to another. Back on Earth, they'd trained on a simulated version of this world. After a lot of false starts, Dash, Piper, Gabriel, and Carly had gotten it done.

But only by cheating.

"Let me guess," he said wearily to Lord Garquin. "We've got to get across the moving plates and into one of those tunnels."

"Indeed," Garquin said. "The tunnels will carry you deeper into the complex, until you reach its heart."

"And how are we supposed to *get* to the tunnels?" Dash asked.

Even Gabriel looked nervous. "Yeah, this isn't a holo-gram. This time, if we fall off a plate or get zapped by a slogger . . ." He peered over the ledge they stood on—the complex went down into the ground just as far as it went up. If they fell, they'd be falling for a *long* time.

Gabriel slid a finger across his throat. "No do-overs," he said. "No cheating."

"Maybe a little cheating," Lord Garquin said. "I know these patterns well. I can guide you across."

Gabriel was watching the moving plates intently. "But there are no patterns," he said. "It's random. Every time it seems like there's a pattern, it switches up."

"What looks random to you, human, is perfectly or-dered to a more superior intelligence."

"Who are you calling *human*?" Gabriel said, sensing he'd been insulted.

"You can really get us across?" Dash cut in quickly. If Gabriel's pride got dented, they could be here arguing all day.

"I really can," Lord Garquin assured them. "The com-puting devices you wear around your wrist each put out an electrical signal—I can track your motions precisely. As long as you do exactly as I say, you'll remain intact."

"Do you think he still counts it as intact if we have a big laser hole blown through us?" Gabriel whispered.

Piper cleared her throat. "Uh, guys? There's just one little problem. Or . . ." She gestured at her air chair. "Kind of a big one."

"Oh." Dash felt like an idiot. Of course Piper couldn't jump from one plate to another. The air chair might be a miracle of technology, but there were still some things it couldn't do. It needed something solid beneath it to hover over.

Piper hated admitting that most of all. But she wasn't about to let her pride get in the way of the mission. "It's okay," she said. "I can just stay here. Guard the entrance."

"You'll do no such thing," Lord Garquin boomed. "Note the girders extending from where you stand to the central column."

The Alpha team duly noted the girders. A network of steel bars sloped dramatically up toward the column, supporting its weight.

"I see no reason you can't ride one of these girders exactly where you need to go."

Piper grinned. "You're totally right!"

"Hold on a second, Piper," Dash said. The girders were less than a foot wide. "How do you know your air chair can balance on those? What if you fall?"

"What if I don't?" Piper asked, and before he could answer, she thrust the chair forward.

"Go, Piper!" Gabriel cheered as the air chair swooped up along the steel slope.

Dash held his breath as the chair tipped and wobbled from one side to another. She was so high up, and if she fell . . .

"What are you waiting for, slowpokes!" Piper slid smoothly over the top of the girder and into the mouth of one of the giant steel tunnels. "Come on up!"

Gabriel shook his head in wonder. "She pretends to be all cautious and practical, but sometimes I think that girl never met a risk she didn't like."

"I'm getting a little tired of risks," Dash said, trying to ease the tension in his chest now that Piper was safe. At least, as safe as any of them were in this place. "Maybe the next element is on a nice quiet planet, with a beach."

"Getting a little ahead of yourself, human," Lord Garquin said. "Let's focus on *this* planet, shall we?"

Dash watched the plates whizz back and forth, and tried to block out the memory of all the times he'd fallen off during the training exercise.

"Ready?" he asked Gabriel. They crouched together, waiting to jump on Garquin's command.

"Ready," Gabriel said confidently.

"Good," Garquin said, "because . . . *go!*"

They leapt together onto the large brass plate that sped past their feet, then rode it until Garquin shouted, "Go again, on your left!"

"Now stop!"

"Go! Go again! Again! Stop!"

They jumped; they waited; they jumped again; they leapfrogged from one plate to the next. It was like the world's most stressful game of Red Light, Green Light.

One quick jump to the left and then another plate zoomed across at eye level. "Duck!" yelled Garquin, but Gabriel was a half second too late. The plate skimmed his head, knocking him off balance.

Gabriel teetered, but Dash grabbed his waist and held.

"Whoa, that was clo—" Gabriel started, but Garquin interrupted.

"In five seconds, leap as high as you can, and grab hold."

"Grab hold of what?" Dash asked as Garquin counted down.

There was no answer, only ". . . three, two, one, go!"

Dash and Gabriel leapt as high as they could.

Dash stretched his arms wide, reaching, hoping . . .

"Yes!" His fingers wrapped around a thin metal bar. He clung tight.

Gabriel hung beside him.

They were hanging from the bottom rung of a metal ladder that climbed up the outside of a steep steel tunnel. Their feet dangled over an abyss.

"Now what?" Gabriel grunted, his grip slick with sweat.

"Now you join your friend," Garquin said.

Dash craned his neck up to see Piper and her air chair hovering at the top of the ladder. Way up.

"Easy for you to say," he grumbled, pulling himself up painfully, one rung at a time. His arms burned with the effort. It's a good thing STEAM bullied them into sticking with their daily training regimen.

It was a long way down.

Finally, Dash managed to pull himself up enough rungs to get his feet on the ladder. Gabriel was one step behind him. Slowly but surely, they climbed. Up and up, until finally, they joined Piper back on solid ground. If you could call the mouth of a giant tunnel suspended a hundred feet above the floor *solid.*

"What took you so long?" Piper teased, grinning.

Neither Gabriel nor Dash had the energy to respond.

"You're welcome," Lord Garquin said in their ears.

"You're seriously overestimating our gratitude," Gabriel said. He rubbed his sore shoulders. Dash was right, he thought. A beach planet wouldn't be so bad next time around. Some tropical smoothies, a little surfing, no carnivorous beasts or snotty aliens with superiority complexes.

"Onward," Garquin said. "Your task is to reach the hub at the center of the complex. There you will find what we both need."

"Yeah, your spy slogger, PETAL," Gabriel said.

"TULIP," Garquin corrected him.

"And you're sure that thing can get the Magnus 7 for us?"

"I'm sure that if you succeed in shutting down the communications hub, I will direct you on achieving your own goals."

It wasn't the straightest answer in the world. But it was obviously the best they were going to get.

"This place is a maze," Piper said as they crept deeper into the tunnel, which quickly forked into three corridors. "How are we ever supposed to find our way?"

"Have no fear," Lord Garquin assured them. "I will get you where you need to go. Now, find the third corridor on your left and follow the tunnel until it branches, taking the fork on your right."

Dash, Piper, and Gabriel followed Garquin's instructions step by step. One turn after another, they made their way deeper and deeper into Lord Cain's kingdom. It was a labyrinth of brass and steel. At Garquin's command, they slithered through narrow tubes and climbed more cold metal ladders that seemed to stretch to the sky. They scaled a steep wall by climbing a knotted iron vine. They trudged down stairs for what felt like a mile, then slid down a twisty, slippery silver chute for what felt like another.

It was like the universe's most ridiculous ropes course. Or maybe some creepy carnival fun house.

They saw no sign of Lord Cain or any other living creature. They passed only sloggers, hundreds of them. Sloggers carrying lava from the river. Sloggers returning to the river to get more. Sloggers doing repairs, sloggers carving out new tunnels, sloggers building more sloggers. None of the sloggers seemed to notice they were there.

Dash couldn't help but worry what would happen if they suddenly did.

"I don't like this," Piper said, hovering across a narrow chain-link bridge. The platforms it connected were only a few yards apart—but the chasm beneath their feet was several hundred feet deep. She muted her MTB's receiver. "Even if Garquin can get us in, what if we need to get out on our own? I don't know about you, but I have no idea how to do that."

Dash couldn't argue. He'd been trying to pay attention to their route, but they had taken so many twists and turns, memorizing the steps was impossible. He didn't know how Garquin could do it from memory.

Of course, that was assuming Garquin wasn't just making it up as he went along.

"This place doesn't make any sense. It's like some wacky fun house of machinery," Gabriel said, tiptoeing across the bridge and arriving safely on the other side.

Dash snorted. "You noticed?"

"No, the way it's designed doesn't make sense." He'd been following their path carefully, trying to figure out the logic of the place. But it didn't have any. And that wasn't logical either. Aliens who were smart enough to build all these robots and a city-sized factory to hold them should have been smart enough to build a factory that made sense. "All these tunnels that don't go anywhere? Or that go everywhere except where you'd want to be. Think about it, we're going to the communications hub, right? Why would you want to make it so hard to get there? Why would you make people go up and up forever and then take a big slide back down again?"

"Because slides are fun?" Piper suggested. "If all it takes to get out of here is a big slide, I'm not complaining."

"No, he's right," Dash said, thinking about it. This route reminded him of the tubing in the *Cloud Leopard*. Sure, you could go straight from point A to point B, but where was the fun in that? The *Cloud Leopard* was designed to let you take the long way around, if you wanted to. That had surprised Dash, and he'd asked Chris about it. Chris's answer was simple: "Why build something boring when you can build something interesting?"

"Maybe this Lord Cain just likes playing games?" Dash suggested. The platform on the other side of the bridge led into another corridor. Its steel walls were so shiny they could see their reflection. Dash sighed and led his team inside. He unmuted his MTB. "Lord Garquin, how much farther do we have to go?"

There was no answer. Dash checked the Mobile Tech Band. Everything looked intact. "Garquin?"

There was a burst of static in his ear. Then it was drowned out by a flood of laughter—but that wasn't coming from the radio. It was almost as if it was coming from . . .

"Are the *walls* laughing at us?" Piper asked.

They were. Also the floor, and the ceiling. The laughter was coming from all around them. And Dash was pretty sure the joke was on them.

"Did someone say something about games?" The voice surrounded them. Dash felt goose bumps rising on the back of his neck. The voice was almost like Garquin's, but it was somehow *off*. It was too cold, too eager, almost joyously cruel. It giggled. "I do *looooove* games."

"Lord Cain, I assume?" Dash said, trying not to panic.

"I know you can hear me, Garquin," Lord Cain's voice said. "No, don't bother trying to answer. I've jammed your communications. I don't think we need to hear from you anymore. I just wanted to thank you for sending me some friends to play with. Maybe you can have them back someday, if I ever get bored." There was another giggle. It sent a chill down Dash's spine. "But I'm very good at amusing myself."

"You know what you were saying about finding our own way out?" Dash whispered to Gabriel. "Now may be the time."

"In a hurry," Gabriel agreed. They turned back toward the bridge.

A steel wall slammed down, inches from Dash's face, blocking their way back.

"NOT SO FAST."

At those words, another wall slammed down, blocking their way forward.

They were trapped in a steel box.

There was no way out.

"Lord Cain, we're sorry for trespassing," Dash said quickly. "We're not trying to get involved in your war, we're just here on a mission for our own planet, we—"

"Oh, I know all about your mission," Lord Cain said. "I know more about why you're here than you do. But now you're here for only one reason. To entertain me."

"So you think it's funny to scare a bunch of kids?" Piper said defiantly.

"I think it's very funny." The evil laughter kicked in again.

"Well, I think that's pathetic," Piper spit out.

Gabriel tapped her on the shoulder. "Maybe don't insult the guy who can crush us like bugs?" he suggested quietly.

"I'd listen to your friend if I were you," Lord Cain boomed.

"And if I were *you,* I'd have better things to do than mess around with a bunch of kids who are just trying to help out their planet," Piper said, her face pink with fury. Dash admired her . . . even as he kind of wished she would stop talking.

But Piper was too angry to stop. If some power-hungry alien wanted to squash her, then maybe she couldn't stop him. But she could at least tell him exactly what she thought of him and his dumb planet. "We're risking our lives to do something that matters," Piper said. "We've come all the way here, millions of light-years from our home, and all we want to do is take a little bit of

Magnus 7 from your river that you'll never miss, and what happens? We get sucked into some ridiculous fight between you and some guy who's probably exactly like you—and I bet you don't know what you're fighting about anymore either. So go ahead and laugh, because this is all just some stupid game to you. But you know what? I feel sorry for you. Because you don't know what it's like to actually care about something that matters. To care about more than winning some *game*. You probably never will."

Even Piper was surprised by all the words that spilled out of her mouth. And in the long silence that followed, she wondered whether she had just made a terrible mistake. Would the others blame her for whatever Lord Cain did next?

Then Dash gave her a small smile. She'd spoken the truth. Whatever happened next, he was impressed by that.

"Ah, you think games don't matter," Lord Cain said finally. "Let's see about that. We'll play a little game, and if you win, you get your chance to accomplish your mission. If you lose . . . well . . ." His laughter echoed against the steel walls. *"NO MORE CHANCES."*

The floor beneath them lit up with color. Rows and rows of glowing colored tiles, each one blue, red, green, or yellow. There was a flash of light, and then the walls each turned a color too. One was blue, one was red, the other two green and yellow.

"What kind of game is this?" Gabriel shouted.

"We can figure this out," Dash said, his mind spinning furiously. All these colors, they reminded him of something . . . but what? "We just have to think."

"Best think fast," Lord Cain suggested. As he spoke, glowing red numerals lit up on the ceiling.

10:00

As Dash stared, the numbers changed.

9:59

9:58

It was a timer. And it was counting down.

There was a loud buzzing noise. Dash gaped at the wall in front of him, the one glowing red, thinking he was imagining things. *Hoping* he was imagining things.

"Am I crazy, or is that wall moving?" Gabriel asked.

Their steel box was shrinking. If they didn't solve this puzzle quickly, they'd be crushed.

"Ticktock, ticktock." Lord Cain chuckled. "Time's running out."

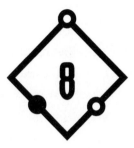

8

"**Aren't you done** yet?" Anna asked, glaring at her second-in-command.

Siena bent over the slogger's control panel, slowly picking through the tangled nest of wires. "Not yet," she murmured, trying to focus. Colin had given her a complicated set of instructions for how to reprogram the slogger to obey their commands. This little robot was one of the most intricate pieces of machinery she'd ever seen, and she was determined to get it right.

"Well, hurry it up!" Anna snapped. They were deep in the heart of Lord Garquin's domain. Colin had assured them that they'd be safe. "Garquin won't hurt you," he'd promised as he steered them through the maze of corridors toward the slogger they needed to find. "He doesn't have the nerve."

Anna didn't like having to rely on Colin's word. If he was wrong, if the sloggers turned on them, they were done for.

"For all we know, the Alpha twits have the element

already," she said impatiently. "They could be heading back to their ship."

"Colin would tell us if that happened," Niko said.

"Colin only tells us what he wants to tell us," Anna countered, and no one could argue with that.

"Do you think maybe Dash had a point?" Siena said as she soldered two wires together. The slogger let out a long, unsettling beep. Hopefully that meant she was on the right track.

"Impossible," Anna said. Then, "A point about what?"

Siena hesitated. She had a feeling Anna wouldn't like what she was about to say. And she'd learned it was easier not to say things Anna didn't like. Still, this had been bugging her all day. Siena only spoke when she had something important to say. But once she thought of that something important, she had to spit it out. No matter who it annoyed. "When he said we could work together to get the elements," Siena said. "Don't you think maybe he was right? The elements are what really matter, and working together offers us better odds to accomplish our mission."

"Says who?" Anna challenged her.

Siena looked up at the team leader, confused. "What do you mean?"

"Who says working together is better?" Anna said. "Do you have scientific evidence of that? Do you have statistics? Hard data? No? I didn't think so."

Siena and Niko were both looking at her now like

she was a little bit nuts. But that only made Anna more certain of her point.

Niko cleared his throat. "I'm not saying we should team up with them or anything," he said. "But you've got to admit that if we cooperated—"

"No!" Anna snapped. "I don't have to admit anything." She'd been hearing this kind of thing her whole life, and she was tired of it.

Two heads are better than one.

Cooperation is better than competition.

Work together and we're all winners!

They were pretty slogans, but as far as Anna was concerned, that's all they were. Slogans. Comforting sayings designed to make people feel better about being too weak to make it on their own. Because the people who didn't believe in competition were almost always the people who knew they couldn't win.

Anna knew she *could.*

Make that *would.*

Teachers at school always tried to pretend that everyone was equal, that everyone was special. That working as a group was better than working alone. But at home, Anna's father had taught her that a group was only as strong as its weakest member. Which is why it was always safest to be a group of one.

He'd taught Anna to care about being the best—about *winning.* And winning meant relying on herself.

"Competition brings out the best in people," Anna

said. "Racing against the Alphas is going to make us a lot faster and better than teaming up with them ever would. Especially because if we *did* team up with them, they'd only bring us down. You remember what they were like back at Base Ten."

"Always swapping secrets with each other. Sucking up to Commander Phillips," Niko recalled, sullen at the thought of it. He still hated that he hadn't been picked first for the mission.

"They did care a lot about getting people to like them," Siena admitted. Talking to people, especially strangers, was hard for her. Making friends came naturally to people like Dash and Piper. They always seemed to know exactly what to say. Siena somehow always said the wrong thing. But so what? She was smarter than any of the kids on the *Cloud Leopard.* That wasn't bragging; it was the simple truth. Just because they were more fun, more charming, more *likable,* did that mean they deserved to be on the mission any more than she did?

"Exactly," Anna said. "That's not how you get things done. It's how you waste time. Let the Alphas do their thing, and we'll do ours."

"Done!" Siena said proudly. She peered down at the slogger, trying to decide where its face would be—if it had a face. "Ready to do what we say?"

The slogger beeped twice.

"Sounds like a yes to me." Niko patted him on the head. "Guy's kind of cute for a tin can, don't you think?"

Anna shuddered. No one knew it, but she hated machines, especially the kind that could understand what she was saying—or talk back. This planet was a horror show of machinery, and she couldn't wait to get back to the ship. "Let's get this thing down to the river and get out of here."

A troop of Garquin's sloggers stomped past them as if they weren't even there. Anna didn't like the looks of them or the looks of the laser cannons sticking out of their chests.

Niko groaned. "Don't know why you're in such a hurry to get back. You miss *him* bossing you around?"

He had a point. Anna had spent her whole life letting her father tell her what to do. Now she was millions of light-years away from home—and, thanks to Colin, still stuck doing whatever she was told. But as the leader, Anna felt like it was her duty to enforce some kind of discipline and respect on her team. (Also, if she let them talk about Colin behind his back, who knew what they'd say behind hers.) "Colin just wants what's best for the mission," she snapped, "and if you feel the same way, you'll get going."

"Bossed around up there, bossed around down here," Niko murmured. Siena swallowed a laugh.

Anna gave them both a sharp look. "What was that?"

"Nothing," they said in unison. The slogger beeped.

The three Omegas made their way back toward the edge of the complex, edging across catwalks and crawling along narrow girders. It was slow going, but Lord Garquin could have made it much slower, if he'd wanted to. Anna didn't understand why he wasn't trying harder to stop them. She knew Lord Cain was throwing everything he had at Team Alpha to slow them down. It didn't make sense that Lord Garquin wouldn't do the same. And Anna *hated* things that didn't make sense.

"Report your status," Colin ordered through their earpieces.

His face glared up at them from the small view screens attached like claws to the back of their hands.

"We've found the slogger you told us about and we're heading back down to the river," Anna reported, pretty sure he already knew that. He could monitor their progress step by step, through their MTBs. "Should have the element in hand within the hour."

"It's seven thousand degrees Fahrenheit," Colin said. "I suggest you keep it out of your hand."

"It's a figure of speech," Anna said. "You know about those, right?"

There was a disapproving silence. Anna swallowed hard. She was officially in charge of the mission, but if Colin ever wanted to demote her, he could. He was the only one who knew everything about their ship and the elements they needed—he could do pretty much anything he wanted.

"Sorry," she said, hating the taste of it.

"Hey, what's happening with the Alpha team?" Niko asked, trying to change the subject. It was weird to see Anna, of all people, trying to suck up to someone. She was really bad at it, and you could tell it was killing her. Maybe she was human after all?

Anna gave him a grateful smile, then quickly wiped it off her face. Gratitude was just another way of showing weakness. Her father had taught her that too.

"No need to worry about the other extraction team," Colin said. "They're otherwise occupied."

Siena frowned at Niko. *Otherwise occupied?* What was that supposed to mean?

"Is it really possible they don't know what's really going on down here?" Siena asked Colin.

"Not everyone's as generous with information as I am," Colin said. "You should thank me for being so open and honest with you. Because unlike some people, I trust you."

"Yeah, trusts us not to get in his way," Niko muttered.

"What was that?" Colin snapped.

"Nothing," Niko said quickly, promising himself to stop muttering things that could get him in trouble.

"Uh, Colin?" Siena said hesitantly. "The Alpha team . . . they're not in any danger down here, are they? Slowing them down, that's fine. But they're not actually going to get hurt, right?"

"Would you care if they did?" Colin asked. He

sounded genuinely curious. "They're your opponents. Anything that happens to them is good for you."

Siena was shocked. She knew Colin wasn't like other people—to say the least. But Dash, Piper, and Gabriel were just trying to do the right thing.

"I wouldn't want anything to happen to them," Siena said firmly. "None of us would, *right*?" She looked pointedly at her teammates.

"Obviously," Niko said. It hadn't even occurred to him to worry for the Alphas. Until now.

The two of them turned to Anna, waiting.

She rolled her eyes again. But she'd figured out that being a team leader sometimes meant sticking with her team. "Agreed, Colin. We don't want anything bad to happen to Team Alpha." As if anything bad was going to happen to Team Twit. They were the four luckiest kids on Earth. Luckier than Anna, at least—how else could they have beaten her out for a spot on the official mission? Certainly it wasn't because they were *better*.

"Hmm." He sounded like he was considering it. Then, "Understood."

The signal went dead.

Siena frowned. "Do you believe him?"

"What? About not hurting the baby Leopards?" Niko said. "Yeah. Of course. Well . . . probably?"

"Not just that," Siena said. "Everything. He knows so much we don't, about the ship, about the mission—our whole lives are in his hands. Can we trust him?"

Many nights on board the *Light Blade,* lying awake, Anna asked herself the same thing. And night after night, she came to the same conclusion. "It's like you said, our lives are in his hands," she pointed out. "So we don't have much of a choice."

9

"**Dude, the walls** are closing in!" Gabriel shouted.

"I noticed!" Dash shouted back. "Why are we shouting?"

"I thought it might make me feel better!" Gabriel shouted, louder this time.

"Did it?"

Gabriel sighed. "No. I still feel like a juice box about to get squished."

"There must be a way out," Piper said. "We just need to think."

They thought.

The walls and floors glowed with color.

The timer ticked down.

They thought harder.

"Fifteen tiles across," Gabriel murmured. His lips were pursed, his tongue poking out just slightly. It was his thinking face. "Eighteen tiles long."

"Better make that seventeen," Dash corrected him as

the room buzzed and the walls chomped up another foot of space. Something about these colors was familiar to him. The buzzing too. It was scratching at the back of his mind, just out of reach.

"And it's all random," Gabriel said, scanning the tiles, searching for some kind of pattern in the dizzying array of color. There was none.

There *was* some kind of structure here, Gabriel could feel it. The problem was, he couldn't *see* it. And if he didn't see it fast, he was going to be a pancake. He slumped against the yellow wall.

"Whoa!" Dash yelped as the yellow flared bright. "What was that?"

Piper hovered toward the green wall and stretched out a hesitant finger. The moment she made contact, the green flared.

"This has got to be part of it," Gabriel said excitedly. "Part of the game."

Suddenly, Dash punched a fist in the air. "Simon!" he shouted.

Gabriel and Piper looked at him like he was losing his mind. Gabriel pointed at himself, then Dash. "Me Gabriel. You Dash. No Simon here."

"No, *Simon,*" Dash said, adrenaline flooding through him. He *knew* this whole setup had seemed familiar. "It's some old game my little sister got from a yard sale."

"And that helps us how?" Gabriel said dubiously.

"It's got colored tiles that light up," Dash said. "Red, green, blue, and yellow. Sound familiar?"

"But what do you do with them?" Piper asked urgently.

Dash tried to remember. Abby had played with the Simon game obsessively for about a week. Then Dash got so tired of its beeping that he stole it and hid it under his bed. After a few days, they'd both forgotten it existed. "It's like Simon Says, but with colors, I think," he said slowly. "A bunch of colors light up in a random order, and then you have to remember it and hit the colored tiles in the same order. If you get the pattern wrong—"

There was another loud buzz, and the walls moved in again.

"—it buzzes!" Dash said triumphantly.

Now the room was only fifteen rows by sixteen. And the timer was down to six minutes.

"So if we hit the right walls in the order of the tiles . . . ," Gabriel mused. It made sense. "But there are two hundred and forty tiles—that'll take forever."

"Maybe it's just one row?" Piper said. "Every time the walls move in, a row disappears. So maybe that means we get a chance to try the next row. Until . . ."

"Until there aren't any chances left!" Dash said in alarm as the walls buzzed and moved again. "And if we don't move fast enough, it must count as a wrong turn.

So let's do it!" He dashed toward the yellow wall to hit the first color in the pattern, then across the green, then back to yellow, then red twice, then—

The walls buzzed, and the row disappeared.

"This is crazy," Dash complained. "The room is way too big to get this done in time."

"It won't be for long," Gabriel pointed out in a gloomy voice.

"Let's all do it," Piper suggested. "I could take the yellow wall. Dash can take the green one."

"I can stand in the corner and get red and blue from the same spot," Gabriel said, getting excited. This could actually work.

"Okay, *go!*" Dash said.

It was total chaos. Dash touched the green wall and Piper hit the yellow one, but then Gabriel hit the blue one before she could hit the yellow one a second time, and all too soon . . .

BZZZZZZ.

"This isn't going to work, not unless someone's in charge," Gabriel admitted. "Dash, you do it."

"What?" Dash was surprised. Did Gabriel really just say that? Gabriel was usually the last person to want him in charge.

BZZZZZZ. The walls seemed like they were moving faster now. Almost as if Lord Cain knew they'd figured out the rules and wanted to make sure they didn't win.

Actually, Dash thought, it was probably *exactly* as if Cain wanted to make sure they didn't win.

"You call out the colors," Gabriel said. "We'll hit the walls in order. Come on, hurry!"

Dash focused on the next row. "Blue, blue, yellow, red, blue, red, yellow, yellow, green, red—"

BZZZZZZ.

"What happened?" he asked, irritated. "Who didn't hit the—oh." He'd been so intent on calling out the colors and watching the walls light up that he'd forgotten he had a color of his own to take charge of.

"Forget it," Gabriel said. "I'll just do it."

"Wait," Piper said. "It's not his fault—it's too confusing to call out the colors and have to remember your own color. Dash, you stand in the middle of the room. Gabriel and I can each take a corner. We can each hit two walls from the same spot."

BZZZZZZ.

"Okay, but if we're going to do this thing, let's do it *fast*," Gabriel urged them. There were only two minutes left on the timer.

It took a few more false starts—once Gabriel forgot that red was on his right and blue was on his left. Once Dash said yellow when he meant green. All the colors were starting to look alike to him.

They tried not to get mad at one another.

And they tried not to notice that the walls were closing in. Only six rows left. Thirty seconds.

BZZZZZZ.

BZZZZZZ.

BZZZZZZ.

"Red, yellow, yellow!" Dash shouted frantically, trying not to trip over his words. "Red, green, blue, yellow, red, red, red, yellow, green, red, green, yellow, *YESSSSSSSS.*"

The lights all flashed at once, blindingly bright. Then the whole room went dark. Dash couldn't see anything— and he couldn't breathe.

What if they hadn't made it in time?

What if this was it?

"Sorry, guys," Dash murmured. He didn't know whether he was saying it to his crew, for getting into this mess, to his mom and his sister back on Earth, or to his entire planet, for letting them all down.

He just knew he was sorry.

"Cain's the one who should be sorry," Gabriel crowed. "Sorry he picked the wrong team to mess with. Look!"

He pointed at a wall, which was slowly but surely sliding up into the ceiling.

They were free.

"Yes!" Dash cried, pumping his fist in the air.

"In your face, Cain!" Gabriel shouted.

Piper was apparently the only one who remembered that they were still trapped in the middle of an alien over-lord's mechanical kingdom. They'd solved one puzzle and saved themselves from getting smashed—but that

91

didn't exactly make them home free. "Um, guys, maybe instead of celebrating, we should, you know . . . get out of here. *Now.*"

"Great idea, Piper," Dash said. "Except . . ."

Except, without Lord Garquin to guide them, they had no idea where *here* was.

Dash deflated. "We're totally hosed," he said. It was surely only a matter of time before Lord Cain decided to throw another "game" at them. "I really am sorry, guys. I should never have gotten us into this."

"We all agreed," Piper said firmly.

"Yeah, but I'm the leader," Dash said. "If we get stuck in here forever, it's going to be my fault."

"Shhh," Gabriel hissed.

"No, it's true, this is my responsibility—"

"No, I mean, *shhhhh,*" Gabriel said. "I'm trying to listen."

There was a long silence. Then— "Listen to what?" Piper whispered.

A satisfied smile crept across Gabriel's face. "Power," he said. "And I can hear it."

"What do you mean?" Dash asked.

"All the power it takes to run this place? It puts out kind of a hum," Gabriel said.

"I don't hear anything," Dash said.

"Me neither," Piper agreed.

CLOUD LEOPARD | PERSONNEL

FIRST NAME	CHRIS
LAST NAME	Unknown
AGE	16?
DATE OF BIRTH	Unknown
GENDER	M
COUNTRY OF ORIGIN	Unknown
GUARDIAN(S)	n/a
GUARDIAN CONTACT	n/a
RECRUITMENT CENTER	n/a
CREW POSITION / TITLE	Ship Specialist - Alpha Team

TEAM ALPHA

FIRST NAME	ROCKET
GENDER	M
COUNTRY OF ORIGIN	Shelter Rescue
GUARDIAN CONTACT	Base Personnel
CREW POSITION / TITLE	Spirit Companion

"Just trust me," Gabriel said. He could hear the complex humming like a lullaby. And he knew if he followed that sound as it got louder and louder, he'd reach its electronic heart. The place that generated all the energy. Probably the place they'd find Cain's communication hub—and TULIP, the spy slogger who would get them all out of here.

Dash and Piper looked skeptical.

"Look at the walls," Gabriel said, pointing at the lengths of cable winding between the dials and gears. "See how they get thicker in one direction, and they kind of branch off in the other?"

"Uh, sort of?" Dash said, in a voice that meant *no*.

"Trust me," Gabriel said again. "This place is nothing but one giant machine. And I *know* machines."

"What about"—Piper pointed up at the ceiling— "you know, him?"

As she spoke, a line of sloggers marched by. Dash got an idea. He stripped off his Mobile Tech Band, then gestured for Piper to take hers off too. "This is how Garquin followed our signal earlier, right?" he whispered. "So . . ." He hoped they would get it. He didn't want to say any more, in case Cain could listen in on their conversation now.

Piper grinned and handed over her MTB. Gabriel kept his but switched its power off. That way, if they ever did get out of here, they'd have some way to communicate with the ship.

"Here goes," Dash muttered, and crept up behind one of the sloggers. The MTBs had a magnetized strip—they stuck perfectly to the back of the slogger's head.

Have fun tracking us, Cain, he thought.

Then, quietly as they could, he and Piper followed behind Gabriel. Gabriel followed the hum of power.

They burrowed deeper into Cain's nest, weaving left and right, following the tunnels and corridors into the heart of the beast.

Finally, they reached a large doorway. Even Dash noticed the hundreds of cables snaking beneath it. Gabriel tapped the door and gave them the thumbs-up.

This was the place.

Dash eased the door open, revealing an enormous domed chamber. It was nearly stadium-sized, its walls lined with displays and switches. Long steel girders supported a massive column at its center. The column stretched from floor to ceiling, every inch of it covered in screens. Each screen showed a different part of Cain's complex. At the base of the column sat a shimmering throne, encrusted with gold.

The throne wasn't empty.

The creature was nearly ten feet tall and seemed to be made of shadows, blurry and flickering at the edges. He had no face; he swallowed the light. He was terrifying.

He was Lord Cain.

And he was flanked by nearly a hundred sloggers. All of whom turned toward Team Alpha as they entered the room. All of whom obeyed their master when he barked out a single word: "Attack."

The door slammed shut behind them.

The sloggers advanced.

It turned out those muzzles poking out of the sloggers' chests *were* laser guns.

And this time, they fired.

Gabriel, Dash, and Piper ducked behind a large bank of servers. They could hear the sloggers clomping toward them. They were slow, and they were clumsy, but there were a lot of them.

And there was no escape.

"What now?" Gabriel said.

Dash had no answers. He'd failed his team. He didn't know how they were going to get out of here. He didn't know how the three of them could defeat a hundred sloggers and Lord Cain. He didn't know whether the sloggers would fry them to a crisp or just trap them so Lord Cain could do something worse.

He didn't want to find out.

The sloggers rounded the corner on their hiding place. Laser shots zapped and sparked all around them.

One thing, at least, was clear.

"Now we *run*!" Dash shouted.

Piper skimmed away from the sloggers, her air chair much faster than their stumpy metal feet. Dash and Gabriel raced in the opposite direction, laser beams sizzling toward them—it was safer to split up. Dash and Gabriel were faster than the sloggers too, but the sloggers were machines. They would never tire.

They would never give up.

"Dash, behind you!" Gabriel shouted, and Dash dove out of the way. The shot missed him by an inch, maybe less. He spun around to see a line of sloggers advancing. They nearly had him surrounded.

"Over here, you clumsy tin cans," Gabriel called, crouched behind a large silver console. The sloggers turned toward him, a second of distraction that let Dash slip away. But now they had Gabriel in their sights, firing as they marched toward his hiding spot. "Great, I got their attention," Gabriel mumbled. "Now what?"

"Hey, sloggers!" Dash yelled. "Slog this!" He grabbed a rusted old bolt from a pile in the corner and threw one as hard as he could at the slogger closest to Gabriel. The pitch was low and fast, perfected in a hundred baseball games back on Earth. The bolt thudded into the slogger and knocked it onto its side. Its shot fired wild, slamming into another slogger. The wounded machine sizzled and sparked, its own laser beam firing out of control.

Dash threw another bolt and then another, knocking down more sloggers. One whirled around, spraying the room with its laser. It was a chain reaction of chaos. Slogger after slogger took a hit, sparking and screeching. Laser shots careened toward the ceiling and burned holes in the machinery lining the walls. Dash raced over to the console where Gabriel crouched.

"Nice one," Gabriel whispered, giving him a high five. The slogger army was tearing itself to pieces. "Where'd you learn to do that?"

"You're looking at last season's MVP," Dash boasted. "I'm missing the All-Star game for this."

"At least this is way more fun," Gabriel said as a monitor exploded over their heads.

"Yeah. Way more."

"Focus!" Lord Cain boomed at his sloggers. "Fire at the enemy, not yourselves!" But it was no use.

"Wait, where's Piper?" Dash asked, alarmed to realize he couldn't see her anywhere.

Gabriel craned his neck, scanning the control center for her. There was a glimmer of movement in the corner of his eye. He caught his breath and nudged Dash. "Up there," he whispered.

Piper had easily sped out of the sloggers' reach—but there was nowhere to hide, and there was nowhere to *go*.

She couldn't exactly crawl under a piece of equipment and hide until the robots gave up looking. Thanks to the bulky air chair, she couldn't hide much of anywhere.

At least—not anywhere on the ground.

And that's where the sloggers had to stay: on the ground. Piper, on the other hand, had options.

As Dash played pitcher with the sloggers, Piper rode the narrow steel girders supporting the central column. Just as she'd done before. And when she rode them all the way to the top, safe from laser beam fire and sloggers and whatever Lord Cain could throw at her, she had time to look around.

She spotted something interesting.

Something near the top of the central column that looked like a large red switch.

This was the communications hub, and Lord Garquin had told them there was something here that could shut down Lord Cain's control.

If I were the main power switch, where would I be?

She thought she'd be up high, out of anyone's reach, for safekeeping.

She thought she'd be big and red, so as to say *important, stay away.*

She looked down at Gabriel and Dash, trapped by a storm of sizzling laser beam fire, and thought: *What's the worst that could happen?*

She leaned out of the air chair as far as she could

without falling. She stretched her fingers as wide as they would go. The very tip of her middle finger found purchase on the red switch.

She flipped it.

"Noooooo!" Lord Cain screamed—and then vanished.

The sloggers stopped in their tracks.

It was as if someone had yanked out their batteries. They stood motionless, waiting for further commands. Dash and Gabriel couldn't believe it. One second, a ten-foot-tall creature of shadows had been cackling down at them—the next second, the throne was empty. The sloggers were harmless. They were safe.

"It must have been a hologram," Piper said, gliding back toward the ground. They'd seen plenty of those back at Base Ten. The holograms had been terrifying, even when you knew they couldn't hurt you. Maybe this one couldn't either—but she was glad she didn't have to find out. "The real Lord Cain's probably miles away. And now there's nothing he can do to us."

"Thanks to *you!*" Dash said, giving her a celebratory fist bump. "You saved our lives."

"That was amazing, Piper," Gabriel agreed, switching his MTB back on. "You're a rock star."

Piper could feel the heat rising to her cheeks. "It was nothing," she said. "Anyone could have done it." But they all knew that wasn't true. Only Piper could have done it.

And that made her feel so good she didn't even mind that her face was probably red as a tomato.

"It was everything," a familiar voice said in their ears.

"*Lord Garquin?*" Dash said in surprise. He'd pretty much given up on the guy.

"Piper has disabled Lord Cain's control over the interior of his kingdom," Garquin said. "He can't jam my signal anymore. We can continue where we left off."

"That's it?" Dash asked, incredulous. "Don't you even want to know if we're okay?"

"Yeah, or how about thanking us, for risking our necks for you?" Gabriel complained. "Cain almost turned us into pancakes!"

"I'm sorry," Lord Garquin said, and he sounded surprisingly sincere. "You've done me a great service today, and for that I thank you. But I assumed you would be eager to continue, since now it's *your* mission that you may turn to. I am eager to repay you."

"Oh. I guess that's okay, then," Dash mumbled. Between the smashing and the running and the army of sloggers, he'd almost forgotten what they were here for. "So what do we do? How do we find this slogger you say can help us?"

"It should be somewhere in the hub with you. Look for the TULIP marking across its torso."

"Shouldn't be hard to find her," Gabriel said. "There's only about a million of them, and they all look alike."

Piper addressed the robots. "Are any of you named TULIP? Come forward now, please."

Gabriel looked at her like she'd lost it. "Uh, Piper, they can't actually understand you."

"How do you know?" she asked.

Gabriel turned to Dash for backup. Dash shrugged. "Worth a try," he said.

"Well?" Piper prompted them. "It's okay, TULIP. We're friends."

They waited. None of the sloggers moved.

"They're just machines," Gabriel said. "They only do what they're told. That's the beauty of machines. Come on, let's go find our girl."

They wove through the throne room, examining the sloggers one by one. Many of them had symbols emblazoned across their torsos. Some looked like the ruins of a complex ancient language, while others were silhouettes of familiar items—a fish, a star shape, two pumpkins. But no tulip shape anywhere.

"All these things look the same," Gabriel complained. "Hey, Garquin, what's so special about this TULIP? Can't we use any of them?"

"The sloggers are controlled by a signal sent out by the central processing unit—they're part of a hive mind, not one of them able to act on its own. You can't reprogram them, because there's not enough there to reprogram," Garquin explained. "But I built TULIP to be special. She's designed to act on her own, even make her own decisions about how to fulfill her overall mission. So with my instruction, you should be able to reprogram her to serve your purposes. No others, only her."

So they kept searching.

"This is taking a long time—do you think the Omega team already has the element?" Piper asked worriedly.

"It's not a race," Dash said. But he didn't really mean it. If Anna Turner was involved, it was definitely a race. And he intended to win. He started to move through the sloggers faster, skimming the symbols written across their metal casing. And then, finally, at the center of a small group of sloggers on the far side of the dome—

"Found her!" Dash cried. He patted Garquin's spy slogger on the head. She had a very clear picture of a tulip flower on her middle. Then he realized what this cluster of sloggers had been working on when the signal died. He swallowed hard. "Uh, guys," Dash said, his mouth dry. He couldn't believe what he was seeing. "I found something else too."

Piper and Gabriel scurried across the throne room to join him.

"Whoa," Piper breathed.

Gabriel blinked quickly. "Am I seeing what I think I'm seeing?"

The sloggers had been building something, a strange, jagged sculpture made of scrap metal. It was a sculpture of a giant face, half-covered by scaffolding, its features stretching nearly twenty feet high.

Gabriel didn't understand. "I mean, is it just me, or does that look kind of like . . ."

Piper told herself it must be some weird coincidence, but you didn't have to be a statistics whiz to know the chances of that were a zillion to one. *"Exactly* like," she confirmed.

"It's definitely him," Dash said, looking back and forth between the sculpture, the sloggers, and the empty throne. He felt like he sometimes did when struggling over a particularly tough math problem. There was some missing variable here, some key that would make everything fall into place. He just couldn't figure out what it was. "It's Chris."

Carly was going stir-crazy. She'd tried everything she could think of to boost the strength of the communications signal. Nothing had helped.

With no way to contact her team, she'd scoured the library archives looking for something that would answer her questions about the *Light Blade.* Who could have built it? What was its purpose? How did Anna manage to chase them halfway across the universe? But there were no answers. Even if there were, Carly wasn't sure she could concentrate enough to notice them. She'd even tried taking a break and playing her guitar, which usually calmed her down. But she had to stop when the music started reminding her too much of home.

She couldn't think about that now—she had to focus

on her crew, down on the planet. Part of her was a little jealous. After all, they were down there exploring, seeing amazing sights, completing an important mission. While she was up here, twiddling her thumbs and waiting for something to happen.

Not that she had anyone to blame for that but herself.

She sighed and forced herself to turn back to the ship schematics one last time—and gasped. There, buried in the exact same diagrams she'd studied a thousand times before, was the answer she'd been looking for. A way to divert power from the navigational system to double the signal output.

Carly leapt up from the chair and dove into the tube portal. She couldn't wait to see the look on Chris's face when he heard that she'd found their answer!

"Wooo!" Carly cried, whooshing toward the bridge. When the others were around, she tried hard to be as mature as she could. After all, she was a crew member on the world's most advanced spaceship, on a life-or-death mission to the stars. It was a grown-up kind of job, and as she was the youngest on board, she always tried to seem especially grown up. But on her own, speeding down roller-coaster hills and around hairpin turns so quickly that her stomach soared into her throat, she let down her guard.

She leapt out into the navigation deck feeling better than she had all day. Her mood plummeted when she re-alized the bridge was empty. Chris had promised to stay there and monitor communications with the planet, in case they came back online. Where could he have gone—and why? Chris was always disappearing off to hidden corners of the ship, which was usually fine. But these weren't usual circumstances.

Fuming, and just a little freaked out, Carly opened a comm line to Chris's quarters. She was planning to tell him the good news; she wasn't trying to eavesdrop. But he must have accidentally left the line with the bridge open on his end, because Carly could hear everything going on in his quarters. And he was talking to *someone*.

"Pay no attention to the statue!" Chris ordered. "I am Lord Garquin, and I command you to focus on the issue at hand."

Now Carly was *totally* freaked out. The ship was empty . . . wasn't it? So what was he doing? "Um, Chris?" she said into the comm. "Who are you talking to?"

There was a long silence. "Carly?"

"Yeah. Carly. The only other person on board. *Right?*"

"Give me a second, Carly," he said. Then he sighed, like he was giving in to something. "I'm coming up."

It only took a minute or two for him to make his way to the navigation deck, but the wait was endless.

Finally, Chris stepped onto the bridge. He looked utterly calm. But then, he always looked calm. It drove Carly nuts.

"How much did you hear?" he asked.

"I heard you talking to someone, which is weird. I heard you call yourself Lord Garfunkel or something like that. Which is weirder."

Chris started to interrupt, but Carly talked over him. It wasn't like her—but then, it wasn't like her to suddenly feel this angry. The words poured out. She couldn't have stopped herself if she'd wanted to. "I know you were lying before about the *Light Blade*—I *know* you know more about that lookalike on the ship than you're letting on. So don't lie to me again. Just tell me, Chris. What's going on? *The truth.*"

Chris wasn't looking so calm anymore—he looked more like an animal caught in a trap. "Now's not a good time for that, Carly."

Something in her wilted. She realized she had been hoping he would deny it. Would say, "Are you joking, Carly? It's me, Chris, maybe not the most forthcoming guy you've ever met, but there's no way I'd straight up lie to you." She'd always known there were things Chris wasn't telling them. It was obvious to everyone that he had his secrets. But she'd thought she could trust him. She'd thought he had the mission's best interests at heart.

Now she wasn't so sure.

And she was getting less sure by the second.

"It's always a good time for the truth, Chris."

He didn't have to tell her. She couldn't make him. She couldn't make him do *anything*, she suddenly realized. He knew much more about this ship than she did, than any of them. Knowledge was power, and he had all of it.

It was crazy to be afraid of Chris.

But one tiny, shivering part of her really was.

Maybe he saw it in her eyes. Maybe that's what convinced him.

"Spill it, Garquin," Dash insisted. Twenty minutes later, and he still couldn't take his eyes off the sculpture of Chris. Or was it the Chris lookalike from the *Light Blade*? It didn't make any sense that Lord Cain would direct the sloggers to build a giant metallic replica of either of them. Not unless there was something very big that Dash didn't know. "Why is there a sculpture of our crew member glaring down at Lord Cain's throne room? What's going on?"

"This is going to take a bit of time . . . ," Lord Garquin began.

"You said yourself, we're totally safe in here," Dash pointed out. "As long as we don't flip that main switch, Lord Cain can't do anything to us. Or was that a lie?"

"No . . . *that* was true," Garquin said. The way he said it made it clear that many other things he'd said were not.

"So just tell us already," Gabriel insisted. "And if you

don't, maybe we'll just turn that switch back on and get the story from Lord Cain."

"You really don't want to do that," Lord Garquin said.

"How do you know what we want to do?" Piper asked. "You don't know anything about us."

"That's not exactly true," Lord Garquin said. "And I suppose that's the first thing I have to admit to you. I'm not Lord Garquin. At least, not exactly."

"Then who are you?"

That's when Carly's voice piped in. "Go on, tell them."

Dash started in surprise. "Carly? But I thought the atmospheric interference—"

"Yeah," she said. "So did I. Turns out we thought wrong. About a lot of things. Starting with . . ."

"It's me," Lord Garquin said. And then his strange voice transformed into something much stranger. At the same time, much more familiar. "Chris."

There was a moment of silence as the shock of it descended on them.

Gabriel found his voice first. "Er, could you maybe be a little more specific? Chris who?"

"Chris who do you think?" Carly said.

"Well, I know it couldn't be Chris, *the guy on my crew who swore he wouldn't keep any more secrets from me,*" Gabriel said. "And it's definitely not Chris, *the guy with no sense of humor,* because this would be a pretty elaborate practical joke."

"Come on, Gabe," Piper said. "Let's give him a chance to explain himself."

"Nothing that comes out of his mouth is the truth," Gabriel said. "And you want him to say *more*?"

"Yeah, I do," Dash said, firmly enough that Gabriel finally let up. "I'm sure Chris has a good explanation for all this . . . right?"

"I have an explanation," Chris said. "Whether or not it's a good one—that will be for you to decide." He paused, as if trying to figure out where to begin. "I told you I was Lord Garquin because, in a way, it was true. Everything you see on this planet, every machine, every slogger, everything—I built it. I first came to this planet nearly a century ago. As you are now, I was searching for Magnus 7 and trying to develop a way to synthesize it into the fuel I needed. In the meantime, to amuse myself, I designed a game. Much like your video games, except this one was the size of a planet. I created Lord Garquin, and Lord Cain too. I set them at war with each other."

"And you didn't think you should mention this a little sooner?" Gabriel said.

"If I'd told you the truth about Meta Prime, it would have raised any number of questions. So I spoke to you with Lord Garquin's voice—but only because you needed me to help you navigate the world."

"Wait, did you say you were here a hundred years ago?" Piper said, confused. "That's impossible! You can't be much older than fifteen."

"To the contrary, I can be much, much older than fifteen," Chris said. "Centuries older. And I am."

"But how is that possible?" Gabriel asked.

Dash's mind was racing. This was it, the missing variable. This was the thing that made everything else make sense: the super-advanced technology on the *Cloud Leopard,* which only Chris knew how to use. That he'd supposedly helped invent, even though he was a teenager. The reason Commander Phillips trusted him so much in the first place. The fact that he'd been on this planet—on *any* planet—before, all those years ago. And had built a game elaborate enough to look like an alien civilization at war.

The fact that he'd lied about it, over and over again.

"He's an alien," Dash said. There was a long silence. Dash could tell from the look on Piper's and Gabriel's faces that they thought it was the craziest idea they'd ever heard . . . and the only one that made sense. "What do you say, Chris? Am I right?"

"You are," Chris admitted. "I'm from another planet, in a far corner of another galaxy. I look human—but I am very much not."

At those words, four minds shared a single thought. *Whoa.*

Dash was the one who'd figured it out—but even he couldn't believe it was true.

All this time, there'd been an alien in their midst?

A creature from another planet, who looked human and pretended to be their crewmate, their friend?

An *alien,* from *outer space.*

Dash thought he'd wrapped his head around the whole alien thing when Lord Garquin started speaking to them—but a voice in your ear was one thing. *Chris,* an extraterrestrial? That was another thing altogether. That was like a cosmic practical joke, and Dash was afraid if he opened his mouth, he'd start laughing and never be able to stop.

Gabriel was shaking his head hard, as if to shake the thought out of his head, to say *no, not possible, not in a million years, not an alien, not Chris.*

Finally, Piper spoke. "Carly?" she said in a strangled voice. "You okay up there?"

Piper was the first to think of it, but very quickly they all started to worry. Carly was up there on the *Cloud Leopard,* alone with an alien. An alien they apparently knew nothing about, who'd been lying to them for months. An alien who had control of every part of the ship and could do whatever he wanted.

None of them knew Chris, not really. They couldn't know what he wanted.

They certainly couldn't stop him from getting it.

"I'm . . . uh . . . I'm okay" came the answer. Dash had never heard Carly sound so uncertain.

"So, you're an alien," Dash said, trying to sound

casual. Like his mind wasn't blown to bits by the idea. "An *alien*. Does Commander Phillips know?"

"He does," Chris said. "He's known almost all his life."

"So how come he didn't tell *us*?" Gabriel said.

"He thought it would be better for you not to know," Chris said. "At least not until you needed to."

"I'll bet he did," Gabriel muttered. There seemed to be a lot of stuff Phillips didn't think the *Cloud Leopard* crew "needed" to know. It was amazing how even when you were picked to go on a mission across the universe to save the planet, most grown-ups still thought of you as *just a kid*.

"I don't get it," Gabriel continued, just warming up. "If you're an alien, what were you doing on Earth? Where's your home planet? Are there more of you? What are you doing on this mission in the first place? And how come you've known Phillips for so long? What were you doing on Earth? Did I ask that already? Is this one of those Superman things, where your world blew up and you're the only survivor?"

Dash was used to the fact that talking made Gabriel feel better. Still, he wished Gabriel hadn't asked that last question. Or at least that he'd phrased it more tactfully. After all, if Earth blew up and Dash was the only survivor, he'd probably be a little touchy about it.

But Chris only laughed. "That's a lot of questions, Gabe," he said. "I'm going to have to start from the beginning."

Piper caught Dash's eye and tapped the TULIP slogger's head. Dash knew what she was trying to say. They were kind of in the middle of something—did they have time to sit around and listen to a long story? Dash wasn't sure. He wasn't sure of anything.

"My planet is called Flora," Chris said, his voice gone soft at the thought of it. "Located in the galaxy you refer to as the Large Magellanic Cloud, one hundred and sixty thousand light-years away from Earth, it is a planet with an atmosphere and planetary crust very similar to your own."

"It makes sense, then, that your people would evolve along the same lines we did," Piper said.

"Exactly. But we've had much longer to evolve, and since the invention of Gamma Speed—"

"Wait a second," Gabriel interrupted. "*You* guys invented Gamma Speed?"

"Of course," Chris said. There wasn't a hint of boasting in his voice. He spoke matter-of-factly, like it should have been obvious. "Surely you didn't believe that humanity could leap so far ahead in such a short time, not without a little help?"

"It's happened plenty of times before," Carly said defensively. She suddenly felt like she—and the whole human race—had something to prove. "Atomic power. Computers."

"The internal combustion engine," Gabriel added. "The wheel."

"We built ships that got us across oceans," Dash pointed out. "Planes that got us into the sky. Shuttles that got us to the moon. And we did all that without anyone's help."

"I don't know why you'd assume such a thing," Chris said. Then quickly added, "You may disregard that. It was simply my attempt at a joke, to lighten the mood."

But once the words were out there, Dash couldn't help wondering: *Was* it a joke? Or was Chris not the first secret alien visitor to Earth? Not the first to inject a little extraterrestrial technology into the veins of humanity? Did Einstein get a nudge from some little green men? Did Darwin? Copernicus? Newton? The possibilities boggled Dash's mind. He couldn't decide whether it was depressing to imagine that the human race couldn't get anywhere without alien help—or astounding.

"Long ago, I left Flora on what was meant to be a hundred-year research voyage."

"*A hundred years* out in space?" Carly yelped. She was already starting to get claustrophobic on the *Cloud Leopard* after only a few months. She couldn't imagine volunteering to spend a lifetime wandering through the stars.

"Voyages of this length are typical for my people," Chris explained. "As you can see, we age at a much slower rate than humans. Our lives are long, and many of us choose to fill them with as many new sights, new places, new peoples as we can."

"So you came to check out Earth, and you liked it so much that you stayed?" Gabriel guessed.

"Not exactly. About forty years ago, your Earth time, a young astrophysicist picked up what he believed were signs of alien life. Specifically, he detected the exhaust from my ship. He was smart and ambitious, and determined to have contact with an alien life-form. I had no immediate plans to visit Earth. But he lured me with a series of distress calls—and he succeeded."

"So this guy fooled *you*, super-advanced, hyper-intelligent alien space voyager?" Gabriel asked.

"I'm afraid he did."

Gabriel thought it sounded like a pretty dirty trick. But he couldn't help being a tiny bit impressed.

"My ship was damaged upon landing," Chris continued. "And so I was stranded on your planet, at the mercy of this astrophysicist, Ike Phillips, who wanted to use my knowledge and technology for his own advancement."

Ike Phillips? Gabriel mouthed at Dash, who raised his eyebrows.

"He didn't care how it might benefit his species or his world. He dreamed of power and profit—the more he could accumulate, the better. He kept me secret on Base Ten, where I have lived for the last several decades."

"But Ike Phillips doesn't even run Base Ten," Dash pointed out. "*Shawn* Phillips is in charge."

"Indeed he is. *Now.* Ike's son Shawn grew up in my company. We became what your people might think of as family. And unlike his father, Shawn cares about helping his planet. When the power started going out, he and I came to see that we might have the solution to the energy crisis."

"You're the one who told him about the Source," Dash guessed, his mind racing. Phillips had never mentioned his father, but there'd been whispers around the base, stories of the stern commander who'd once been in charge. If he was anything like Chris said, it was hard to imagine him raising a son like Shawn. "And you helped him build the *Cloud Leopard* so that we could go and find it."

"Yes, Dash. This mission is something Shawn and I dreamed up together. It has been my privilege to join you on it, to see these dreams come to reality."

"So you just want to help the people of Earth out of the goodness of your heart," Carly said.

"I do."

"Even though we lured you down under false pretenses, and ruined your ship, and kept you prisoner for the last forty years." She snorted. "Yeah, I can totally see why you'd love us."

"Ike Phillips is only one man," Chris said. "Not all humanity."

"Sure, that's what you say now," Gabriel said. "But you've been lying to us this whole time, so who's to say you're not lying now?"

"We don't know that he's lying," Piper pointed out, trying to be fair.

"Thank you, Piper," Chris said.

"Of course, we also don't know that he's telling the truth," she added.

"That's everything?" Carly said. "There's nothing else we don't know?"

Chris sighed. "There are a great number of things you don't know. The things you don't know about the universe, about my people, about your own, they would take several lifetimes to learn. There is no such thing as knowing everything. There is only knowing enough."

Chris was so good at answers that said nothing, Dash thought. He hadn't minded it so much until now. He hadn't thought about all the things Chris *wasn't* saying.

"I assure you that you can trust me," Chris said. "You must trust me. Especially now, on this planet. I created all civilization on Meta Prime, I know it inside and out—I can get you off safely, with the element you need. Once you're back on the ship, I can answer all your questions and more."

"Here's one you should answer right now," Gabriel said. "If you created this place, and you're on our side, how come Lord Cain was doing his best to kill us?"

"I . . . well . . . it seems I've lost control over the Cain side of the planet. Originally I believed it might simply be malfunctioning," Chris admitted.

"But now?" Gabriel prodded him.

"But now I suspect that the person they call Colin, on the *Light Blade*, must be at the controls."

"The one that looks like you," Dash said. "The one you said you'd never seen before."

"That was true," Chris said. "But Ike Phillips had many opportunities over the years to extract samples of my DNA. Given Colin's appearance, given the similarities between his ship and our own, I can only surmise that Ike created a clone of me—one that has my memories, and my knowledge. It is somewhat disconcerting."

"You think Ike Phillips is the one who sent the *Light Blade* after us?" Dash said. "He doesn't sound like the kind of guy who's all that interested in saving the world."

"No," Chris said. "I don't believe him to be that kind of guy."

He paused to let that sink in.

Whoever succeeded in this mission would have the most powerful energy source the world had ever seen, Dash thought. Free renewable energy could improve the lives of every person on the planet.

Or it could improve the life of the person who *controlled* it.

Especially if that person was only out for himself.

"I believe Colin is controlling Lord Cain," Chris continued, "attempting to delay you in your mission to the advantage of his own crew."

"That's pretty sketchy," Carly said.

"I would agree," Chris said.

"And if he's an exact copy of you, doesn't that mean you're pretty sketchy too?" Carly added.

"Even a clone has free will," Chris said. "If everything he knows about life comes from Ike Phillips, I can only imagine the kind of person this Colin has become. He is sure to be ruthless and likely without much respect for the lives and needs of others. So you see, you need my help."

"Assuming we can trust anything you say," Gabriel said. He looked to Dash. "What do you think?"

Dash wasn't just the team leader—he was the one who had gotten to know Chris the best. He was the one who trusted Chris the most. But now he didn't know what he thought.

He only knew how he felt, which was foolish, and betrayed.

And more determined than ever to collect all the elements—and to do it before Ike Phillips's Omega team had a chance.

"I think we can finish this mission on our own," Dash said. "And we can deal with everything else when we get back to the ship. Agreed?"

"Agreed," Piper said.

Gabriel nodded. "Agreed."

"Agreed," Carly put in, though she didn't sound too happy about it.

"Not agreed!" Chris said urgently. "You need me to—"

Dash cut off the radio.

"You really think we can handle this all on our own?" Gabriel asked.

Piper chewed at her lip.

Dash forced a confident grin. "Looks like we're about to find out!"

"Okay, Gabriel, you're up," Dash said. If Gabriel couldn't figure out how to reprogram TULIP to follow their commands, then this mission was a dead end.

Gabriel pulled out his tool kit and pried open the slogger's command panel. "I've never met a machine I couldn't get on my side," he said, studying the complex knot of wires and chips. "No reason to think that's going to change now. And now that I know the same mind that designed the *Cloud Leopard* built this little guy—trust me, I got this."

He sounded confident enough—but as the minutes dragged on, Dash started to get nervous. Gabriel was still just *staring* at the inside of TULIP's head, like he was waiting for a message. Or maybe an instruction guide.

"Are you going to, you know, *do* something?" Dash asked.

"I'm thinking," Gabriel murmured.

"Give him time," Piper said softly. "He'll figure it out. And if he doesn't . . ."

"No," Dash said firmly. The more unsure he was, the more certain he tried to seem. "We're not asking Chris. We can do this ourselves. Right, Gabriel?"

But Gabriel didn't answer. He'd plunged elbow-deep into TULIP's circuitry, clipping and twisting, severing and soldering. TULIP beeped and chittered.

"Sounds like it tickles," Dash said.

"You're not hurting him—er, her, are you?" Piper asked, worried.

"It's a machine," Gabriel reminded her. "It can't feel pain."

"How would you know?" Piper asked. She was used to people making assumptions about her. There were plenty of things people thought she couldn't do—and they were wrong. She knew better than to make that kind of assumption about other people. Even when the people were machines.

"Ask it yourself," Gabriel said, easing the panel shut. "I'm all done here."

"That fast? You really did it?" Dash asked, hope rising.

"Did you ever doubt me?" Gabriel said. "Wait, don't answer that." He patted TULIP proudly on the head. "Go on, girl, tell Piper that it didn't hurt a bit."

TULIP trilled happily.

"And now you're going to help us get some Magnus 7 out of the river, right?"

TULIP trilled again, and to Dash, it sounded a lot like an enthusiastic *yes.*

They couldn't go back the way they came. Without Garquin, they'd have no hope of getting past the moving checkerboard floor. Even if they wanted to open communications with the ship again, they couldn't try the targeted electromagnetic pulse—all the doors to the outside were run by electronics. If they blew out the circuits while they were still inside the complex, they could be trapped there forever.

"Is there another way out, TULIP?" Gabriel asked. "We need to get down to the lava river. But not through the main entrance."

The slogger cheeped happily at him and toddled off down a corridor. Gabriel still didn't believe that a mining machine like this could have a personality . . . but he had to admit, TULIP seemed to like him the best.

He didn't mind.

They followed the slogger through a labyrinth of corridors. They passed hundreds of other sloggers, all of them inert, waiting for Lord Cain's signal to direct them. Piper wondered what they were thinking, if they could think. She wondered what TULIP was thinking, speeding past all her frozen brothers and sisters. Did she feel sorry for them? Piper did. What must it be like, spending your entire life following someone else's commands?

Without Lord Cain around to get in the way, it was simple getting to the outside.

The problems only started when they got there.

Problem number one: TULIP took them out by an alternate route, just like they'd asked. And Dash could see why no one went this way. When they passed through the wall, they found themselves standing on a ledge, two hundred feet above the ground.

Problem number two: They'd cut off Lord Cain's control over the inside of his complex but not the outside. The cannons along the wall were firing and would until they ran out of fuel. Flaming lava balls flew across the river, showering the Alpha crew with a rain of sparks.

But Garquin wasn't fighting back.

"He doesn't want to risk it," Piper guessed. "I bet he won't fire until we're safe."

A single fireball from Lord Garquin's side could have incinerated the whole Alpha crew in one shot.

"Not sure I like betting my life on alien logic," Gabriel said.

Garquin's side was taking a beating. Lava splattered the towering wall, scorching and melting large swaths of machinery. Steel sizzled away, leaving gaping holes in the circuitry. Dash wondered how much the complex could take before it was destroyed.

Piper took a deep breath. It was good to be outside again, under open sky. Even if the sky was lit up by flaming balls of molten lava. "Poor Lord Garquin," she said.

"Uh, did you forget there is no Lord Garquin?" Gabriel reminded her.

"I know, but . . . it feels like there is, you know?"

It was silly, but Dash *did* know. He'd heard Garquin's voice, followed Garquin's directions. It was Garquin who'd gotten them into Cain's complex and helped them find TULIP. And now it was Garquin getting pummeled because he wanted to keep the Alpha team safe. Even though Lord Garquin didn't actually exist, Dash felt a little bad for him too.

"It's not our problem," Dash reminded Piper. Saying it out loud helped him remember. "Or, at least, it won't be as soon as we can get the Magnus 7 and get off this planet. So let's get started."

Piper peered dubiously over the ledge, two hundred feet down. "Are we supposed to jump?"

TULIP squawked at them, then chugged down a narrow ramp clinging to the side of the wall. Slowly but surely, the robot led them through the strange obstacle course that scaled the side of the wall.

"This is insane," Dash complained as he inched precariously across a foot-wide catwalk. "Who would build a pathway like this?"

"Makes a crazy kind of sense to me," Gabriel said. "Now that we know this whole planet is basically one big video game. It's almost fun."

"This is your idea of fun?" Piper said, looking at him like he was nuts.

Gabriel ducked a splatter of lava, then clung tight to the narrow conveyer belt that would carry them down another twenty feet. "Well . . . yeah."

Piper was just glad for her air chair. It was more sure-footed than anyone's legs could be.

Still, she didn't look down.

After what seemed like an eternity, the path forked. To the right, a smooth, curved surface veered steeply down, like a playground slide. To the left, what looked like a million stairs descended toward ground level. TULIP stopped in between, as if uncertain.

"Which way?" Piper asked the robot.

TULIP beeped twice. It sounded like an apology.

"I don't think she knows," Piper said.

"Good thing I do," Gabriel said, pointing at the slide. "I don't know about you, but my legs are killing me, and I'd like to get off this planet before it tries killing me. Again. Slide's faster than stairs, simple."

Dash agreed with Gabriel that the sooner they got back to the ship—and Carly—the better.

"But is it too simple?" Piper argued, wishing she agreed with Gabriel. The air chair could hover down the stairs, but it wouldn't be very much fun. "You said it yourself, if this is a planet-sized video game, it makes sense that everything's so complicated and hard. Why would Chris build in an easy shortcut, so close to the end?"

Dash agreed with her too.

"Uh, because it's *fun*?" Gabriel said. "*You* said it yourself—this place is built to be fun, and slides are officially fun. Definitely more fun than *stairs.*"

"That's a really steep slide," Piper said. "By the time we got to the bottom, we'd be going pretty fast."

"Duh. That's the point," Gabriel said, itching to get started.

"And what are you going to do at the bottom, when you're going so fast you can't stop yourself from—"

"Yeah, from what?" he challenged.

"From, I don't know, from sailing straight into the mouth of some carnivorous beast," Piper suggested, her voice rising.

Gabriel waved it off. "You've got Raptogons on the brain. Wrong planet. Wrong problem."

"Your way's risky," Piper said.

"Your way's slow. And in case you haven't noticed, we're in the middle of a war here. What's riskier than slow?"

"What do you say, Dash?" Piper asked. "Which way should we go?"

"Yeah, oh fearless team leader," Gabriel said. "What's your vote?" Gabriel hated letting Dash decide. Not that he wasn't a great leader—Gabriel couldn't deny he was the perfect guy to lead this mission. But having a leader meant *being* a follower, and he wasn't particularly good at that. It was easier to listen to a suggestion than obey an order.

He was working on it.

"What's it going to be, Dash? Pointlessly hard work, or some good, fast fun?"

Dash didn't answer. They both made sense. How was he supposed to know who was right?

Of course, there was one way: he could ask the guy who built it. The alien who built it.

But no way was he going to do that. No matter what.

Safe in the *Clipper,* the shuttle that would carry them back to the *Light Blade,* Anna, Niko, and Siena watched the fireballs rain down on Lord Garquin's kingdom. Their little slogger was crammed into the crawl space behind the seats, a sample of Magnus 7 safe in his belly. They'd succeeded—and they'd done it a lot faster than the crew of the *Cloud Leopard.*

Down on Meta Prime, Lord Garquin's domain was burning. Thick clouds of billowing black smoke almost hid it from view. Anna wondered how many more hits it could take before it totally collapsed.

"You almost feel bad for the guy," Niko said. He shifted uncomfortably in the seat. The cushioning was so thin you could feel the springs and the metal frame. Nothing about this ship, or the *Light Blade,* for that matter, was built for human comfort. It felt like riding around space in a go-kart. Niko was constantly tripping over misaligned panels, slamming his elbow into half-screwed-in bolts, slicing his palm on sharp edges. Everything felt slapped together at the last minute, like the time Niko hadn't bothered to start his science project until the night before the science fair. That project had, literally, blown up in his face. Niko spent a lot of his time hoping the *Light Blade* wouldn't do the same.

"There is no *guy*," Anna reminded him. "There's just Chris and a bunch of robots."

"Still, look at him, just sitting there, taking it. What kind of wimp doesn't fight back?"

"The kind who'd rather not blast his own crew with a face full of molten lava?" Siena suggested. The three Omegas exchanged a knowing glance. Colin had restrained himself from blasting their side of the river until they'd made it to shelter in the *Clipper*—but then he hadn't waited ten seconds before unleashing his cannon fire. Piloting the *Clipper* through a hail of fire had been no picnic. One of the fireballs had come within inches of searing off their aft thrusters. Not that Colin had apologized. Colin never apologized.

At least he had opened up a narrow flight corridor for them through the firestorm. He assured them that as long as they stuck to his instructions, they would avoid getting blown out of the sky. It had worked—just barely.

"Let's just get back to the ship," Anna said.

"Do you think—" Niko stopped himself.

"What?" Anna asked.

"You're not going to like it," he warned her.

Anna was getting pretty used to not liking things. "Spit it out."

"Do you think we should stick around here for a bit before heading into orbit?" Niko asked. "Just to make sure the Alphas make it back safe?"

"They're not our responsibility," Anna pointed out.

"Yeah, but they *are* the only ones who know where the next element is," Niko argued. "If the Alphas don't make it to the next planet, then neither do we."

"He has a point," Siena said.

Anna hated to agree . . . but she had to. The Omegas had a ship of their own and an alien of their own, but they didn't have a *route* of their own. They had no choice but to follow the *Cloud Leopard* from one planet to the next. Which meant if Dash Conroy screwed things up for the Alpha team, he screwed things up for everyone.

"Fine," Anna grumbled. "We wait."

The *Clipper* carved lazy circles through the clouds, high above the battle raging below. Anna programmed the scanners to latch on to the *Cloud Cat*'s energy signature. When the shuttle took off—if the shuttle took off—they'd know it.

"I still can't believe Chris would send them down to that planet without warning them what they were going to find," Siena said. There was nothing worse than going into a situation without the right set of facts. What kind of person would put his crewmates in that position? "Do you think Colin's right? That Chris just let them believe Lord Cain and Lord Garquin were real? That this 'war' was anything but a game?"

"He must have," Niko said. "What else was he going to say, 'I built the whole thing myself back before you were born, but don't ask me any questions about how I managed to do that or why I still look fifteen, because I'm not allowed to tell you. But I swear, there's a totally good explanation and it has nothing to do with me being an alien'? I think Dash would have seen through that one."

"It doesn't seem right," Siena said.

"Face it, Chris is a liar," Anna said in a hard voice. "Just like Shawn Phillips." Commander Phillips had pretended to be a nice, friendly guy, but she'd never trusted him. There was too much he refused to tell them. All that talk about classified information, top secret, need-to-know—to Anna, it had sounded a lot like an excuse. A lot like the kind of thing grown-ups said when they didn't want you asking the wrong questions. They wanted you to keep quiet and follow orders. Anna's father wasn't like that. He'd raised her to always ask questions. He expected Anna to do as she was told, but he always explained why. He wasn't a "because I said so" kind of guy.

It turned out Shawn Phillips's dad wasn't either.

When a team of commandos had kidnapped Anna and the others on their way back home, Anna hadn't known what to think. But then Ike Phillips had introduced himself and explained the need for the ambush. It was all Shawn's fault, he said. Just like everything else.

"I would have happily approached you more forthrightly," Ike Phillips told them. "I would have worked *with* Shawn to make you the offer of a lifetime. But my son is greedy. He wanted you all to himself—and once he had no more use for you, he didn't like the idea of anyone else stepping in to give you what you want."

"And what is it you think we want?" Anna had asked, boldly speaking for the group.

"I think you want to go into space," Ike Phillips said. "I think you want to save the planet, and get rich and famous doing it. And if you agree, I'm the man who can make that happen for you."

Then Anna had known *exactly* what to think: *YES.*

Just like the Alpha crew, they'd gotten a ship full of wonders and six months of training. Unlike the Alpha crew, they'd been told the truth about their ship and their mission.

"My son, Shawn, believes in coddling people," Ike had told them, just before takeoff. "Especially kids. Not me. I don't believe in treating people differently just because they're young. I always held my son to the same standards as anyone else. Childhood is no excuse for immaturity. I believed that then, and I believe it now. You four, you claim you're smart enough and tough enough to pilot my ship across the universe—does that mean I can trust you to be mature? To handle the truth, no matter what it is?"

Anna, Siena, Niko, and Ravi had nodded. Of course, they would have agreed to anything that would get them on that ship.

"My son is going to lie to his crew. The Alpha team, 'best and brightest of the world's youth.'" At that, Ike had laughed cruelly. The crew of the *Light Blade* liked the sound of that. They laughed too. "But you four? I'm going to tell you the truth."

Ike had told them the whole story. How an alien had crash-landed on Earth many decades before. How Ike had saved his life, nursed him back to health, and this alien, Chris, had betrayed him. "Turning my own son against me!" Ike exclaimed, shaking his head in wonder and despair. "Conspiring to force me out of my own program? To force me into exile? After everything I did for him?"

Shawn simply wasn't qualified to put together such an important mission, Ike had said. "He's my son, and of course I love him, but the fate of the planet is at stake. He and Chris are simply incapable of leading Project Alpha. Look at the four crucial mistakes he's already made!" He pointed in turn to the four Alpha rejects. Each of them shone under his gaze. Each of them thought, *Yes, Shawn Phillips made a huge mistake not picking me.*

Ike Phillips had given them a chance. Ike Phillips had

given them the *Light Blade*. He'd given them his trust, by telling the truth about the *Light Blade*'s alien technology. And he'd given them Colin.

Sometimes, Anna wished she could give that particular gift back.

13

Carly strummed her guitar, picking out the melody of an old Beatles song that made her think of home. It felt a little strange to be playing here, on the navigation deck. But there was no one to hear her but Rocket. STEAM was off puttering around in the galley, directing the ZRKs on a big welcome-home meal for the crew. "Of course they're coming home!" the robot had told Carly. "You gotta have faith, yes sir, you do!"

Carly was glad at least one of them had it. Maybe STEAM could have enough for the both of them.

She didn't ask STEAM if he'd known Chris was an alien. After all, Chris was the one who'd designed the robot. Which meant either they could both be trusted—or neither of them could.

After Dash cut off communication with the ship, Chris had locked himself away in his quarters. Carly didn't know what he was doing in there. She tried not to worry about it.

She let herself sink into the music, and the memories

it played through her mind. Her father, adjusting her fingers on the frets and showing her how to hold the pick. Her little sisters, begging her to play some J-pop or Taylor Swift so they could sing along. Her mother, rubbing lotion onto Carly's hands, fussing over the calluses that her father said were the sign of a true musician. He'd been a musician himself once, and he'd put a guitar in Carly's hands before she was old enough to walk. He liked to say that her first words were the lyrics to "Hey Jude," and she could never be sure he was joking.

Carly hadn't spoken to her family since she'd said good-bye to them, back on Base Ten. They sent videos sometimes, but seeing her mother grinning and waving, seeing her father cook her favorite meals, seeing her sisters playing laser-pointer tag with the cat . . . it was almost worse than not seeing them at all.

The guitar usually calmed her, but now it was no use. The familiar melody only reminded her of how alone she was in the stars, alone on this ship.

Alone except for Chris.

There was a knock on the wall behind her. Carly set down the guitar and turned. Chris stood before the tube portal. "May I join you?" he said.

"You can do whatever you want," Carly said, and they both knew it was true.

He took a seat beside her at the controls. "Any word?" he asked.

She shook her head.

She didn't know how she was supposed to act. Carly knew all about aliens—at least, the fictional kind. It's not like you took a class on aliens in school, shoved in there between algebra and gym. Carly knew about Thor and E.T. and all the weird creatures in Star Wars. She knew about alien parasites that devoured you from the inside out; she knew about alien invaders, whether they were two-headed or elephant-shaped or carnivorous plants. She knew some aliens came to Earth eager for conquest, while others were stranded voyagers from the stars, hoping for a way home. But those were pretend aliens, safely inside a screen or a comic book. Chris was real—and he was right *here.*

139

"I didn't mean to interrupt your playing," Chris said. "It was lovely."

Carly blushed. "Thanks, I guess."

"You're missing home," he said. It wasn't a question.

"What about you?" she asked. "Do you ever miss it?"

"Earth?" Chris said. He shrugged, then gave her a small smile. Carly saw it now, the way his gestures seemed studied, almost artificial. As if he were playing a role. Like he had to think to himself, *This is when a human would shrug. This is when a human would smile.* "I'm used to long journeys," he said. "I focus on what comes next, not what I left behind."

"No, not Earth," Carly said. "Home. Your home. Do you miss that?"

Chris bowed his head. "Oh. My home."

The way he said the word *home* . . . it was like a long, mournful chord. He didn't have to say anything else.

"What's it like there?" Carly asked.

"It is a world of water, much like your own," Chris said, "but our seas are rich green, and their sparkling channels circle the globe. We live on land that curls like a snake through the emerald waters. I wish you could see it, Carly."

"Are there people waiting for you?" Carly asked. "Like, do you have parents? Or friends? Or, I don't know, somebody?"

Chris nodded. "There are many somebodies," he said quietly.

"Do you think they're worried?"

"On my world, we come and go. Long passages of time pass between meetings. They would have no reason to expect my speedy return, and yet . . ."

There was a long pause.

"What?" Carly said.

"I think sometimes, perhaps they miss me," Chris said. "Perhaps they wonder about me, and worry for my safety. But—" He shook his head, as if trying to shake away the thought. "It's best not to dwell on those left behind. The friends of yesterday are no more important than the friends of today."

"Friends don't lie to each other," Carly pointed out. "Especially not about things that really matter."

"You've never lied to a friend?"

"No!" Carly said hotly. Then, without even knowing why, she continued, "Well, actually . . . can I tell you something?" She wasn't sure why she had the sudden impulse to confess to him. Maybe because he wouldn't judge her for it. He couldn't, not now. "I lied about why I wanted to stay on the ship. It was just because I was too chicken to go down to the planet."

Chris nodded. He didn't look surprised. "If you were 'chicken,' you wouldn't be on this mission," he pointed out. "You're risking your life just being here."

"Maybe, but that's a risk I know all about," Carly said. "Once I know everything that might happen, I'm not scared anymore. It's the stuff I *don't* know about. . . ."

"You thought you would be safer on the *Cloud Leopard*, where you knew what you were dealing with," he guessed. "That nothing dangerous or unexpected could happen here."

"Yeah."

He smiled ruefully. "And how has that worked out for you, trapped on the ship alone with a dangerous extraterrestrial?"

Carly laughed. She hadn't thought about it that way. "Not so well, I guess."

"I left behind everything I ever knew, in search of new experiences," Chris said. "Surprises aren't always bad."

"You still think that? Really? Even after crash-landing on Earth and getting stuck millions of miles away from home?"

Chris nodded. "I will never regret this journey, Carly. I never regret the things I've done. Only those I have not."

It made a weird kind of sense. As soon as the *Cloud Cat* dropped out of orbit, Carly had regretted not being on it. And her regret grew and grew every second the crew was out of contact. Afraid or not, she should have been down there with them. Next time, she promised herself, she would be.

If there was a next time.

"You won't tell the others, will you?" she said. "I need them to feel like they can count on me. I know I just gave you a hard time for lying to everyone, but this is different." She stopped for a second, wondering if that was true. "I mean, it's personal."

"You have my word." He paused. "Is that worth anything to you anymore?"

She didn't answer. For a long time, neither of them spoke.

"I'm worried about them," she finally admitted.

"I wish I could tell you not to. But I fear they may be walking straight into a trap. One of my own making."

"Then you have to warn them!" Carly insisted.

"They don't want to hear from me," Chris said. "Dash made that very clear."

"You need to try harder. Convince him." She hesitated. "Like you convinced me."

Chris's smile outshone the Meta Prime sun. "Really?"

Carly felt a weight drop off her shoulders—it felt good to follow her instincts, to let herself trust him. It felt good to not feel so alone. "Really. I know Dash cut the signal, but I'm guessing you have some way to override that. Don't you?"

"Well, now that you mention it . . ." Chris fingered a few buttons on the comm, then drew closer and spoke into the mike. "Come in, extraction team. This is Lord Garquin. I'd like another chance."

"We're wasting time," Gabriel complained. "Let's pick a route and get going!"

"Give me a second," Dash said. He had almost decided they should take the chute. He just wanted one more second to make absolutely sure. "I'm—"

The radio buzzed. "Come in, extraction team. This is Lord Garquin. I'd like another chance." It was Lord Garquin's voice, not Chris's. Dash guessed he shouldn't be surprised that Chris had the technology to disguise his voice. Or to activate an MTB even when the extraction team had turned it off. He wondered if anything could surprise him anymore.

He sighed. "Give it up, Chris," he said into the radio. "I already told you, we don't need your help."

"You don't need Chris's help—but you do need *Lord Garquin*'s help. This is my planet, and you need my guidance if you want to stay alive."

"No, we—"

Piper nudged Dash. "It doesn't hurt to *ask*," she whispered.

"I have the capacity to track all planetary movement," Chris said. "Through your remaining MTB, I can see exactly where you are in Cain's complex, and I need to tell you: you're about to walk into a trap."

"Oh yeah?" Gabriel scowled. "Prove it."

"You're standing on a ledge midway down the wall of Cain's complex," Chris said. "Before you lies a long, steep stairwell and a steel chute that will take you to the ground level."

"So you can spy on us," Dash said bitterly. "Is that supposed to make us feel better?"

"The chute is the most direct route to the surface, the one the sloggers themselves take—"

"*Yes!*" Gabriel pumped his fist. "Right again."

"—but it will drop you directly into the lava river," Chris finished. "The sloggers have a hover capacity that allows them to skim across the surface, much like Piper's air chair. Dash and Gabriel, on the other hand, would be taking quite an unpleasant swim. I strongly recommend you take the stairs."

"There's no reason to think he's telling us the truth," Dash pointed out.

"There's no reason to think he's lying," Piper said.

"I say this to you as Lord Garquin. You have done me a service, as we agreed, and I would like to honor my pledge to get you safely down to the surface and accomplish your mission as well."

It was ridiculous, but somehow thinking of the voice as "Lord Garquin" made it easier to trust. Even though they all knew there was no such person. He *felt* real—and he hadn't steered them wrong yet.

"Stairs?" Dash asked his team. They nodded—Gabriel looking unhappy, but resigned. "Stairs it is."

The stairs were steep and long. They seemed to stretch down and down forever. Piper's air chair skimmed easily along their slope. So did TULIP, though she didn't seem too happy about it. They tromped down one flight after another—then stopped abruptly.

"What was that?" Piper asked.

That was a low rumble, like distant thunder.

"It's probably nothing," Dash said. Though he didn't quite believe it himself. Had Chris sent them into a trap?

Then the stairs started to quake beneath them.

"Uh, that doesn't feel like nothing," Gabriel pointed out as the stairs shook and shuddered.

Dash scrambled around for something to grab hold of, but the walls were too smooth. He didn't know what was happening, but he did know they had to get out of there, *fast.* "I think we'd better—*aaaaaah!*"

The ground dropped out beneath him. The stairs flattened themselves into a slick metal chute, and Dash and Gabriel plummeted down and down.

There was a deafening *whoosh,* and suddenly, Dash felt himself buoyed up by a cool cushion of air.

"It's like the tubes on the ship!" Dash cried, the wind stealing his words out of his mouth.

"Only faster!" Gabriel shouted, shooting past him. "Wooooo!"

Dash felt a surge of pure joy as he whipped along the steep chute, the walls a blur of silvery motion. Gabriel was right, this was several times faster than the tubes on the ship, and he probably should have been frightened, or worried, or preparing himself for whatever came next—but it was too much fun. He couldn't help himself: he gave in to the ride. The chute veered up, down, spiraled upside down, then plunged again. Dash's stomach ping-ponged against his lungs, his face stung from the blasts of air, he didn't know whether to scream or laugh or puke, and he loved every minute of it.

After what seemed like forever and not nearly long enough, there was a rush of warm air at his feet that slowed his motion, and he popped out of the chute, landing on the ground with a soft thump. Gabriel was already there, shaking his head in wonder. Piper and TULIP brought up the rear. "Is *that* what riding the tubes in the ship is like?" Piper asked, her face split open by a wide grin. "No wonder you spend so much time in there."

"They're not like that," Gabriel said. "Man, *nothing*'s like that. Who wants to go again?"

Dash said nothing. All his joy drained out of him as he caught sight of the other chute, the one they'd almost taken. It was dropping sloggers straight into the lava river.

Exactly as Chris had warned them.

Before Chris came on the radio, Dash had been ready to choose. And he would have chosen wrong. He would have incinerated his entire team. He'd been so determined to do things on his own, but why? One bad decision—*his* bad decision—and it would all have been over.

Dash knew that he couldn't let himself second-guess every decision he made. That was no way to lead. It was no way to live. He couldn't let himself think how close he'd come to disaster.

But it was hard not to.

Carly spoke into their earpieces. "What's going on down there, guys?"

"Oh, not much," Gabriel said. "Just the greatest ride in the history of the universe, that's all. You don't know what you're missing."

"Yeah," Carly said, a strange note in her voice.

Before Gabriel could ask her what was up, Chris cut in with new instructions. This time, he used his own voice.

"You're going to need to tweak TULIP's programming a bit more before you collect the Magnus 7. The sloggers are only programmed to hold the molten lava for the amount of time it takes them to transfer it to the factory.

If this programming is not altered, TULIP might well self-destruct before you can make it back to the ship. I will direct you on the alterations."

"How do we know doing that isn't going to make the thing blow up?" Gabriel asked suspiciously.

"Why would I want to blow up my own slogger?" Chris asked. "Why would I want to blow up my crew?"

He had a point.

Dash wasn't about to make the same mistake twice. Maybe Chris wasn't the most trustworthy guy at the moment, but he was their best chance at getting off Meta Prime alive. He'd just proven that. Dash glanced at his team, asking them a silent question.

Piper nodded. After a moment, Gabriel nodded too.

"Tell us what we need to do," Dash told Chris. "We'll do it."

14

Following Chris's instructions to the letter, it only took Gabriel a few minutes to alter TULIP's circuitry again.

Nothing blew up.

"This almost feels too easy," Piper said as they pressed themselves into a crevice of Lord Cain's wall and watched TULIP march toward the riverbank.

"Never say that!" Gabriel warned her. "Haven't you ever seen a horror movie?"

TULIP didn't seem to notice the cannonballs of lava flying overhead. A thin tube protruded from her chest and sucked in the molten lava.

"It's like she's drinking through a straw!" Piper exclaimed. "You think she likes it?"

"I know *I* like it," Dash said, watching in amazement as TULIP's belly lit with an orange glow. A robot full of Magnus 7—he couldn't believe it. They'd actually gotten the second element.

"Two down, four to go," he cheered.

"Never say that either!" Gabriel urged him. "Not until we're safely back on the ship. However safe *that* is."

"When did you get so superstitious?" Dash asked.

"Maybe since I found out the guy I beat in Ping-Pong last week is an ancient alien who built a planet-sized video game that did its best to kill me?" Gabriel said. "I don't know about you, but I'm not going to feel safe until we get off this planet."

"Speaking of . . . ," Dash began. Now that they had the element, there was nothing keeping them here. "Ready to make a run for it?"

"More than ready," Piper said. "Let's get out of here!"

They raced for the *Cloud Cat,* dodging sparks and lava, looking back every few seconds to make sure TULIP was following behind. The little slogger with a belly full of Magnus 7 had suddenly become the most important member of their crew.

Soon enough, they were strapped into the *Cloud Cat.*

"Permission to take us up?" Gabriel said, slipping on his flight glasses.

"Permission more than granted," Dash said, holding tight as the engines roared to life.

The *Cloud Cat* shot off the ground and sliced through the air—then shuddered.

"What was that?" Piper yelped. The air was alight with molten lava as Lord Cain fired everything he had across the river. "Were we hit?"

"I don't think he's aiming at us," Dash said. "I think we're just in the way."

"It doesn't matter who he's aiming at—it only matters who he hits!" Gabriel said as a gush of lava came dangerously close. The *Cloud Cat* bucked beneath them, losing altitude. Gabriel gritted his teeth, intent on finding a path through the fire. "I can't get clear of it." He took the ship into a shallow dive, then veered sharply away from a stream of lava. He searched desperately for empty air, but couldn't find a clear path through the heavy rain of artillery. The shuttle bobbed and weaved, but it was no use. Globs of molten lava splattered the hull. The shuttle's control panel started flashing red.

"Don't panic," Dash told him, his own heart thumping a million times a minute. How much of this could their little shuttle take? "Just stay calm, you got this."

"Of course I got it," Gabriel said, but he wasn't so sure. They needed to get above the fighting, into the safety of the alien orange clouds. But the sky was so dense with flame, he didn't know how he could do it. He was going to fail his crew, fail his mission.

"Come in, *Cloud Cat*. Come in!" It was Anna's voice on the comm.

"Not now," Dash snapped as the shuttle took another hit. If this ship was going to crash, no way did he want Anna Turner's gloating to be the last words he ever heard. "We're kind of in the middle of something."

"Yeah, we can see that," Anna said. "You want our help, you have to ask."

"What, you can shut down a war?" Dash asked. Not that it was much of a war. Only Lord Cain's side was firing.

"Oh, just send them the flight path already," Niko's voice said.

"They should say please first," Anna said.

"*Anna.*" That was Siena, and she didn't sound happy.

"Whatever," Anna said. Then, "There's a pattern to the lava ball trajectories. I'm sending you our flight path. Program it in, that'll get you to safety. We're two klicks to your east. You can follow us out of here."

Dash couldn't believe the Omega team was actually trying to help. "How do you even know—"

"You losers want out of here or not?"

"We want out of here," Gabriel said, dodging another barrage of fire from the surface.

The Omegas sent the data packet, and as the ship's computer uploaded the information, Gabriel's view of the sky lit with a glowing route to safety. "Here goes everything," he murmured, steering the ship carefully along the course. His fingers twitched at the touch pad, his gaze riveted to the iridescent trail. The Omega's safe corridor was just wide enough for the ship to pass through the firefight—there was no margin for error.

"That must be them!" Piper cried as a black shuttle came into view. "Anna and the others."

"On it," Gabriel said, all his concentration funneled

into steering the ship. Even with the flight path and the Omega shuttle to follow, this was nearly impossible. Like threading a needle—at a thousand miles an hour. The tiniest of false moves would turn them into a fireball.

The two shuttles sliced through the smoke, up and up, lava scoring their hulls and heat pulsing at their windows, until, finally, they broke into the clouds. The firestorm died away beneath them.

Gabriel let out a breath he hadn't known he was holding. His limbs went weak with relief. "We made it," he said, switching over to autopilot. It was the first time he'd ever been grateful to give up the controls.

"Yeah, and you're welcome," Anna said in the radio. "Maybe next time you should just stay up in orbit and let us handle the tough stuff."

"Oh yeah?" Dash said. "Maybe next time *you* should—"

He stopped when he realized the line had gone dead.

"Also, thanks, I guess," he added. The words were a lot easier to say when he knew Anna couldn't hear them.

The _Cloud Cat_ limped into the _Cloud Leopard_'s docking bay. There would be a lot of repair work to do before the shuttle was planet-ready again. But Dash, Gabriel, and Piper weren't thinking about that as they bounced out of the _Cloud Cat_. They were eager to get to the navigation deck, where Carly was waiting. It felt like they hadn't seen her in a month.

When they made it to the bridge, they found Chris hunched over the controls. Carly was at his side, shouting suggestions.

"Get him on his left flank!" she shouted. "Yeah, and another one! Light that sucker on fire!"

"Everything okay up here, Carly?" Dash asked.

"Fine, fine." She gestured for him to shush. "Let him focus."

"I am very glad you made it safely back to the ship," Chris said, without taking his eyes off the view screen. His hands flew across an elaborate control panel that Dash had never seen before. His fingers were a blur of motion, and with each move, more destruction rained down on the surface of Meta Prime. "As soon as I tie up this loose end, we can be on our way."

Dash grinned. That was just like Chris, to call a no-holds-barred fight to the death a "loose end."

"You really think it's that *Light Blade* guy, Colin, at the controls for Lord Cain?" Gabriel asked.

"I see no other option," Chris said, through gritted teeth. "And I'm going to make him wish he never left Earth. This is *my* game. *My* world. And if he thinks he's going to take it from me? He's sorely mistaken."

They cheered him on. Even Piper got into the spirit. It was impossible not to. They'd never seen Chris so determined—and they'd never seen a battle so furious. Cain and Garquin were unleashing everything they had against each other.

"Go, Chris!" Dash shouted as balls of fire carved an enormous crater in Cain's kingdom.

"Bring it, Garquin!" Gabriel cried as two fleets of sloggers charged the river. They faced off, spewing lava back and forth across the stream of fire.

The fighting stretched on and on. The surface of the planet was littered with scorched sloggers. All across both kingdoms, flames spurted into the sky.

"How will you know when you've won?" Dash asked. "Is there a point system or something?"

Chris glared at the screen. "I win when there's nothing left of him."

"**Yeah, Colin, you** can do it! Blow him away!" Ravi shouted.

"Silence," Colin snapped. "I need to concentrate."

The *Light Blade* crew fell silent. They watched Colin manipulate the controls like a machine. They watched the surface of Meta Prime erupt into flame. It wasn't just lava cannons anymore. Drones swooped through the clouds, dropping bombs that exploded on impact. Sloggers the size of tanks rolled along the river, blasting holes twenty feet wide. Garquin's and Cain's sides were exactly evenly matched. Which made sense, Anna thought, since Chris and Colin were exact copies of each other.

"If you keep this up, you're likely to destroy the whole planet," Siena pointed out.

Colin snorted. "What do you think I'm trying to do?

He thinks he can beat me with his little toy? See how he likes it when I take his toy away." He shifted one of his joystick-like controls and down below, a mile-wide quadrant of Garquin's kingdom turned to ash.

"Seriously?" Niko said. "You don't mean literally, though, right?"

"Yes, Niko, I mean literally," Colin said snidely, without looking away from the screen. When he wanted to, he could make you feel like the world's biggest idiot. "Chris doesn't understand what it takes to win. But he will."

The war stretched on as both sides tore each other to pieces. A whirling storm of fire swirled across the planet's surface. Smoke choked the sky. Metal screamed. Machines twisted and burned. Geysers of flame erupted, spitting columns of lava into the sky.

And then . . . silence.

There were no weapons left to fire.

There were no sloggers left to battle.

There was nothing left on the planet, nothing that could fight. Nothing that could move. Nothing but scorched land and smoldering heaps of twisted metal. Strewn limbs of sloggers torn to pieces. Deep craters of scored and blackened dirt and rolling dunes of ash. Broken, crushed, dead machines.

Everything Chris had built was gone. Meta Prime was nothing but a lifeless rock. The only evidence it had ever been more were the sloggers on the *Cloud Leopard* and the *Light Blade*. The only two who had escaped before the carnage.

Piper thought about how the sloggers had sculpted the face of their master. Did they do that because Lord Cain demanded it? Or was it possible that they had built the sculpture on their own, simply because some tiny piece of them *wanted* to? Was it possible that the sloggers actually had some sentience, a sliver of a mind of their own?

Piper hoped not. Because now they were all gone.

"Did you . . . Do you think you won?" Gabriel asked.

"Of course he won," Carly said. "Lord Cain is dust."

"But so is Lord Garquin," Gabriel pointed out. "The whole planet is dust."

"Guys, stop," Dash said quietly. Chris had left his spot at the controls and was walking slowly toward the wall-sized view screen. He pressed his palm to it, covering up one of the burning piles of rubble.

"It took me four years to build this," Chris said, sounding a little lost. "I was bored and, I suppose, a little lonely. I wanted something to keep me sharp. A game, like the training games you have on the ship. So I built little mazes for myself. Small puzzles to solve and, gradually, larger ones. And eventually, it became more than that. Garquin and Cain, they became real to me. When I pitted them against each other, it was a way for me to push myself. To be better, faster, smarter. But Meta Prime grew to be so much bigger than me. It was an entire world, a civilization. I built it. And—" He turned to face his crew, face pale. "And now I've destroyed it."

"It was *Colin*," Dash said hotly. "It's his fault. You only did it because of him."

"Yeah, what were you supposed to do?" Gabriel asked. "Not fight back?"

"I could have let him win," Chris said. "I could have let him have his victory, and let Meta Prime live on. In all the universe, there was nothing else like this planet. And now there is nothing at all."

15

"**We got the** Magnus 7," Dash told Chris, hoping to cheer him up. "That's the important thing. And we couldn't have done it without you."

It was like he didn't even hear. "I simply don't understand how I got so caught up in the game," Chris said. "Why didn't I stop myself?"

"I get it," Gabriel said. "When you're playing, like, the galaxy's best video game, you're not going to shut it down before you win."

"But to what end?"

"To the end of *fun*," Gabriel said. "You've heard of fun, right?"

Chris shook his head. "I'm supposed to know better."

"Why, just because you're older than us?"

Piper nudged him. "Because he's not *human*," she reminded Gabriel.

"Oh. Right."

There was an awkward pause. In the excitement of

the battle, they had all nearly forgotten what came before. Now Dash looked more carefully at his friend, trying to wrap his brain around the fact that Chris wasn't human. Though maybe he was more human than he thought. After all, weren't they on this mission because humans had got so caught up in having fun—with their cars, their factories, their luxuries of modern life—they'd nearly destroyed their own planet? It just took a little longer.

He studied Chris from head to toe, trying to figure out what he had missed. Surely there was *something* about Chris he should have seen. Something that marked him as nonhuman.

Gabriel and Piper were thinking the same thing. All three of them examined their extraterrestrial crewmate, searching for clues.

"Why are you all staring at me?" Chris asked.

"Are you wearing, like, a costume?" Gabriel asked. "Does the real you have two heads?"

"Gabriel!" Piper said sternly. "That's rude."

"What? How is that rude? Maybe on his planet two heads is the latest trend."

Carly giggled.

"Ignore him," Dash told Chris. "But . . . ah, now that you mention it . . . what *does* the real you look like?" In movies, aliens were always disguising themselves as humans with high-tech camouflage technology. Or brain-distortion fields. Or disguises made out of human skin.

Dash tried not to think about that last one.

"This is the real me," Chris said. "My people look just like your people on the outside. Our planets share certain key atmospheric and mineralogical features that enabled parallel evolution. This is it. No antenna, no third eye, no two heads. I hope you're not disappointed."

"Of course not," Dash said. He couldn't stop staring at Chris. It was suddenly starting to dawn on him: this was a being from another planet. An *alien*. Dash had been so focused on Chris's lies, and the question of whether he could be trusted, that he'd forgotten to be amazed.

Chris was from another planet. Dash's big-brained crewmate was an extraterrestrial.

And when he thought about it, that might be pretty much the coolest thing that had ever happened in his entire life. Which was saying a lot, given everything that had happened lately.

"You could have just told us," Dash said. "You *should* have. Especially when you knew what we were going to face down on Meta Prime. You let us go in blind."

"Why would he tell us the truth?" Gabriel said sarcastically. "So much simpler to just pretend to be a creepy alien overlord named Lord Garquin and make up a whole elaborate fake story to get us where we needed to go. Or was that just more of you having fun?"

"I'll admit, the temptation to take up Lord Garquin's role again was somewhat irresistible," Chris said, and if Dash didn't know better, he'd think Chris was blushing. "You said it yourself, this is the best game in the galaxy."

"Yeah, that part where we almost got creamed by Cain was especially fun," Gabriel muttered.

"But it was also the best way to guide you safely through the planet's obstacles without raising too many complicated questions," Chris said, sounding more sure of himself this time. "I thought it was my best option."

"That's what bothers me," Gabriel said. "You thought lying was your best option then. What about now?" From the beginning, he'd been the most suspicious of Chris, ready to mutiny when the strange older boy first appeared on his ship. "You say you designed this ship—this whole mission. And here you are, risking your life alongside the rest of us. *Supposedly.* Why would you do that if you're not even human? What do you care about saving the Earth?"

"It's true that Earth is not my original home," Chris said. "But I have adopted it as my own. Shawn Phillips is my family. You, all of you, are my friends. The success of this mission matters as much to me as it does to you, because your world is also my world. Does it matter whether we come from the same species? You have confided in me, and I should have done the same in you. I made a mistake—but doesn't that make me more human, not less? Though I can't prove to you that I speak the truth, I will do everything I can to earn your trust back. Right now, in this moment, all I can do is ask you to have a little faith. Believe me. For all our sakes."

It was a pretty speech. But could they afford to be swayed by pretty speeches?

Piper rubbed the smooth surface of her air chair. She'd started to wonder: If Chris was responsible for all the alien technology on the *Cloud Leopard*, did that mean he had also designed the air chair? If she had Chris to thank for that . . . well, didn't she owe him one?

Carly remembered how Chris hadn't judged her for being afraid of the unknown. How could she judge him? Maybe even Chris was sometimes afraid.

Dash hated that Chris had lied to them. But in a way, Dash was lying too, about his age. And if he had his reasons, maybe so did Chris.

"I apologize again for keeping this from you," Chris said. "I made a mistake. You should have known from the beginning."

It was the first time he'd actually said that he was sorry—that he'd flat-out admitted he was wrong.

"As far as I'm concerned, you're officially forgiven," Carly said.

"You're still part of Team Alpha," Piper said.

"Part of the family," Dash agreed.

They all turned to Gabriel.

"What?" he said.

"Don't you have something you want to say to Chris?" Carly prompted him.

Gabriel scowled hard—then broke into a grin. "Oh,

what, that whole alien thing? We still talking about that?" He swatted the topic away. "Forgiven and forgotten."

Carly clapped her hands together, hard. "Then it's agreed. We make this a fresh start. An honest start. No one else on the ship is an alien, right?" She looked from one crew member to the other.

Dash grinned and shook his head. So did Piper.

Gabriel paused. "Well, now that you mention it . . ."

"I'm not counting visitors from Planet Annoying," Carly countered.

"Oh, in that case, one hundred percent human here."

"So can we agree?" Piper asked the crew. "Honesty, from here on out? From everyone?"

"Agreed," Gabriel said. Carly closed her eyes for a moment, like she was making a silent promise to herself, and then echoed him.

"I will do my best not to lie to you again," Chris said.

Dash said nothing. He didn't know what he *could* say. How was he supposed to promise total honesty, when he was keeping such a huge secret?

He hated lying, but he also knew what would happen if he told the truth. The crew would always be worrying about him. Watching for signs that he was weakening, that the trip was taking its toll. He didn't want that. He was their leader.

He had to be strong.

But he also had to be trustworthy.

"You guys, I—" Dash stopped when they all turned to look at him. He cleared his throat. "I, uh, there's maybe something I—"

The insistent beep of an incoming transmission stopped him.

"It's Earth!" Carly cried, bringing their mission commander's image up on the screen. Dash swallowed a sigh of relief. He would still tell them the truth. When they were done talking to Commander Phillips.

Maybe.

"I've been trying to get through to you for days," Phillips said. Communicating over such large distances was always dicey. Even when he got through, his voice was clouded with static and his image froze every few seconds. Still, it was better than nothing. "If all's going according to schedule I assume by now you've made it to Meta Prime and I look forward to hearing . . ." His voice trailed off, as he eyed each of them in turn. His gaze settled longest on Chris. "I see," he said. "You told them the truth about where you came from."

"They figured it out," Chris said.

Phillips shook his head ruefully. "Of course they did. They're the four most capable kids on the planet. I should have known they'd sniff out the truth."

"You *should* have just told us," Dash said. "From the beginning. Instead of lying to us."

"I have never lied to you," Phillips said indignantly.

"Are there things I haven't told you? Yes. Because it's not time for you to know them. I'm the adult here. You're going to have to trust me."

Now Dash was the one getting indignant, and he could tell he wasn't alone.

"You're the adult, but we're the ones flying the ship," he said. He couldn't believe he had to explain this to Commander Phillips *again*. "We're the ones risking our lives. Traveling across the galaxy on the mission *you* charged us with, because you thought we could handle it. So you're telling me we're grown up enough to handle saving the Earth, but when it comes to what we should and shouldn't know, we're just kids?"

"It doesn't sound great when you put it like that," Phillips said, "but . . . yes."

"Is that how your father thinks too?" Dash asked.

Shawn flinched. "What does my father have to do with anything?"

Dash didn't know what to say—none of them did. Was it possible that for the first time, they actually knew something that Phillips didn't? Serious as the situation was, Dash had a hard time holding back a smile. This felt pretty good. "You should probably ask him that yourself," he said.

"Excuse me?"

"Don't worry," Dash said, and set his smile free. "We'll tell you when we decide you need to know." Dash knew he'd have to fill the commander in eventually—the

Omega mission was too important to keep secret, as was Ike Phillips's involvement. But there was no hurry. He could tell, from the overly serious looks Piper, Gabriel, and Carly had fixed on their faces, that the others were enjoying it just as much.

Dash glanced at Chris, wondering if the alien's loyalties to Shawn Phillips would win out over his loyalties to the crew. But Chris said nothing.

"This isn't a joke, Dash. If there's something I need to know, you need to tell me." Phillips was using his sternest "I'm in charge" voice. And he was in charge—but he was also billions of miles away. What was he going to do . . . ground them?

"Exactly," Dash said. "And if you *do* need to know, we'll tell you."

Gabriel snorted. Piper had a hand over her mouth, and Carly's shoulders were shaking with suppressed giggles.

Phillips's face had turned red, and Dash worried he was pushing his luck. "This transmission could cut out at any minute," he said. "And you still haven't briefed us on our next planet."

Commander Phillips treated their planetary excursions like military missions, briefing them on each new destination only once they'd finished with the last one.

"I think that's the most important thing now," Dash said. "Don't you?"

Phillips took a deep breath and composed himself.

Dash knew that he cared more about this mission than anything else. He wasn't going to let anything risk it, especially his own temper. When he spoke again, he sounded utterly calm, as if nothing had happened.

"You'll be traveling at Gamma Speed for ninety-one days, until you reach the planet Aqua Gen. Located in the Tarantula Nebula, it orbits a G-type star, much like the Earth's sun," he said, and continued on with a long list of details about the planet's atmosphere and ground conditions. "I'm sending a data packet along with this transmission," he concluded. "It should contain everything you need to know."

Everything you *think we need to know,* Dash thought. But he only nodded.

The crew all passed along messages for Phillips to give to their friends and families. All except Chris, of course. He never had any messages for Phillips, and now they understood why.

"And now?" Phillips said.

"Now what?" Dash asked innocently.

Phillips gave him a look that Dash recognized. It was the same look his mother gave him when he mouthed off one too many times and got sent to his room without dessert. "You've had your fun, Dash. You've made your point. You all have. Can you please tell me what in the world is going on up there? And what it has to do with my *father*?" His voice twisted harshly on the word.

It wasn't exactly an apology, but Dash suspected it was the best they were going to get.

"Well, to start with, you'll never *believe* what happened when we exited Gamma Speed. . . ."

As Dash walked Phillips through everything that had happened with the *Light Blade* and everything they knew about the Omega mission, Phillips's face turned to stone.

"I'll look into this and get back to you," he said tersely when Dash was done. "I'll let you know what I find out."

Doubt it, Dash thought. But he simply nodded and said, "Yes, sir. We look forward to hearing it."

The transmission shut off. Dash wondered if his friends were thinking the same thing he was: That the Omega mission was a pretty huge thing for Phillips to be clueless about. Especially when his own father was the one in charge. What else didn't the commander know? Add that to all the things Phillips refused to tell them, and it left a whole lot of unanswered questions and potential surprises still to come.

Anything could happen out here, and only one thing was for sure: they would have to face it on their own.

16

The *Light Blade* bounced and shuddered through Gamma Speed. The floor tilted. The lights flickered. The walls stretched and bulged. At times, it seemed like reality itself was fraying at the seams. Anna didn't know any more about Gamma Speed than the rest of her crew, but she knew enough about physics to know how it *didn't* work. Physics said that nothing could travel faster than light. But the *Light Blade* was crossing hundreds of light-years by the day. Which meant it couldn't be traveling through normal space. Anna pictured the needle-nosed ship spearing its way through dimensions. Or maybe the engine somehow folded space-time, as if it were a piece of paper. Fold it in half and smash any two distant points together. For all she knew, the ship flew on fairy dust and magic beans.

But whatever the engine was designed to do, it didn't quite do it. Anna was pretty sure the walls weren't supposed to swell and the floors weren't supposed to sway. She suspected that the crew wasn't supposed to feel woozy for months on end. Sometimes, in Gamma Speed, it felt like her body was being stretched out across the galaxy like a rubber band. She waited for it to snap.

Anna counted the cracks in her dorm room ceiling, trying to fall asleep. She couldn't get used to this room, just like she couldn't get used to Siena's breathing in the bunk bed below. They weren't allowed to put up any decorations, so the room was simply a blank cube. Empty walls, empty surfaces. No pictures of their families. Nothing to make this place feel like hers.

And, of course, it wasn't hers.

It was Ike Phillips's.

It was Colin's.

She bet it wasn't like this on the *Cloud Leopard*. She bet Dash didn't sit around worrying about what would happen if the engine failed in the middle of their journey. If they would be trapped between dimensions or be crushed into galactic dust. Did he even know how close he'd come to being incinerated? Anna had gone out of her way to save him, and he hadn't even bothered to say thank you.

Anna would never let anyone guess it, but she worried about everything. Whether her team would listen to her. Whether Colin would ever stop bossing her around.

Most of all she worried about what would happen if they lost the *Cloud Leopard*'s energy trail. It was like following a trail of breadcrumbs, and everyone knew how that turned out. If the *Cloud Leopard* got too far ahead—

or if Dash found a way to ditch them, to gobble up the trail—the *Light Blade* would be stranded in distant space.

No way forward.

No way back.

Ravi and Niko stared at their screens with glazed eyes. Ravi smothered a yawn. Niko stretched his legs, which were starting to cramp. They'd been sitting in the library for hours, memorizing ship diagnostics and running through simulated malfunctions.

Ravi's stomach rumbled loudly.

"Tell me about it," Niko said softly. "I'm starving too."

"Then let's just sneak out of here and grab some food," Ravi suggested. "Five minutes. No one will know we're gone."

"Colin will know," Niko said.

"That guy is driving me nuts. We've been working and training nonstop. Doesn't he know humans like a break every once in a while?"

Colin had the Omega team on a strict schedule. He dictated when they got up (early), what they ate (flavorless but "nutritional" gruel), and what they did all day: train, study, train some more.

"We do need to learn all this stuff," Niko pointed out. "It'll help us with the mission."

Ravi gritted his teeth and got back to work. Niko didn't get it, how it felt like the walls were closing in on him. Because Niko, at least, had escaped down to the planet for a few hours. While Ravi was stuck up on the ship—stuck with Colin.

"You're not actually going to *do* it, right?" he'd asked as the Alpha kids had struggled to solve Lord Cain's riddle while the walls closed in on them. "You're just messing with them."

"Am I?" Colin had asked, with a smile so creepy Ravi shuddered just thinking about it.

"Let's just finish this," Niko said now. "The sooner we do, the sooner we can eat."

"That's not much to look forward to," Ravi said, thinking of the bowl of disgusting slop he'd had for lunch. "I miss French fries."

"And ice cream," Niko agreed. "Man, I could do with a triple-scoop sundae right about now."

A voice boomed from the speakers built into their screens. Colin's voice. "That doesn't sound like working. Focus!"

Niko and Ravi groaned.

Then they did as they were told.

Siena studied the math problem, scribbling equations in the margin of the page. Puzzling over whether to integrate. Whether the matrices were orthogonal. Whether, if she calculated the eigenvector of A, she could solve for B and x.

She wasn't trying to solve the problem because Chris had told her to or because it would help on her mission.

She was doing math for fun.

It was weird, she knew that. But so what?

Siena knew the others were a little homesick. Back on Earth, she never quite fit in. She liked it better up here, in the dark of space. She liked the quiet. She liked the way priorities were so clear. They had a mission, and the mission was all that mattered. Life was like a math problem. It made sense.

Mostly.

In math, *mostly* wasn't good enough. You couldn't *mostly* understand a principle. You couldn't *mostly* derive a solution.

Siena thought that was true in life too.

So it bothered her that she didn't completely understand Ike Phillips's motives.

That she didn't completely trust Anna to lead the team.

That she didn't trust Colin at all.

She told herself there was no need for concern. One way or another, they would get the elements, they would fuse them together into the Source, and they would get home.

Everything would work out fine.

She told herself that over and over, and she believed it.

Mostly.

Ike Phillips glowered down from the view screen. "You understand how paramount it is to keep the *Cloud Leopard* in your sights, yes?"

"Of course I do," Colin snapped.

"Everything is resting on you," Ike said. "Don't screw this up."

Colin waited until the transmission cut out before rolling his eyes. He supposed he should be grateful to Ike. After all, the man had created him. But the man was obsessed with being in charge.

Colin had learned a lot from Ike, including how good it felt to be in control. And now, with millions of light-years between him and his creator, he finally could be. The *Light Blade* was *Colin's* ship, and the mission was his too. The Omega crew would do what *he* said, or they would be sorry. As the Alpha team would be sorry, if they got in his way.

Let Chris weep and moan about his faraway home-land. Colin shared Chris's intelligence and his abilities, but not his past. Under Ike Phillips's watchful eye, Colin had studied the logs from Chris's ship, and knew nearly every detail of the alien's journey.

Once, long ago, Colin had been jealous of Chris. After all, Chris was the original, Colin was merely the copy. Chris had a history, a life, a whole and independent self. Colin had only what Ike Phillips told him.

But Colin had come to understand that he wasn't simply a copy of Chris, he was an improvement. Because the past only held you back. Colin didn't need one of those. He had a future. Let Chris drown in his pathetic little memories of home. Colin's home was Earth, and when he returned there with the Source, his planet and everyone on it would be his to control.

Ike had taught Colin something else: if you wanted something, really wanted it, you should do everything in your power to get it.

Colin planned to get what he wanted.

No matter what.

The Magnus 7 was too hot to store in the Element Fuser, at least until they had all the elements and were ready to fuse. Instead, TULIP stationed herself beside the fuser. The molten lava would stay in her belly for the rest of the voyage, until they needed it.

Of course, they would only need it if they succeeded.

"Do you think she'll get lonely in here?" Piper wondered.

"Lonely? I won't let that happen, no sir," STEAM assured her. He'd taken a liking to the new robot. "TULIP, I think this could be the beginning of a beautiful friendship, yes sir!"

TULIP cheeped and beeped, and her belly glowed just a little brighter.

"Dude, are you *blushing*?" Gabriel asked her. "You're a machine—have a little dignity!"

TULIP whirred.

"I think she's telling you that she can do whatever she wants," Piper translated.

"Yes indeed," STEAM said. "This is an *A*"—he pointed to himself—"and *B*"—he pointed to TULIP—"conversation, so you can *C* yourself out of it."

A crash of mechanical sounds erupted from STEAM and TULIP. It took the crew a moment to catch on: the robots were laughing.

By the time they slipped back into Gamma Speed, things had finally gotten back to normal. The crew gathered around the dinner table, peppering Chris with questions about his home planet and what it was like to be an alien.

"What is it like for you?" he asked.

"Dude, weren't you paying attention?" Gabriel asked. "*You're* the alien. We're human."

"That makes us aliens to him," Carly pointed out.

The thought stopped everyone cold.

"Whoa," Gabriel said. "Mind blown. So does that mean you want to ask us some questions, Chris? Want to know what it's like to have such puny, feeble brains?"

"Perhaps someday you will show me your third eye," Chris said drily.

"Did everyone hear that?" Gabriel exclaimed. "The extraterrestrial almost made a joke!"

Carly tossed a French fry at him. "I too would like to know what it's like for you having such a puny brain, Gabe."

The others burst into laughter, their tension leaking

away by the second. It felt good to be together like this, all five of them. It felt right. But before the meal could give way to hysteria and a potential food fight, Dash cleared his throat. "We need to talk about something serious for a second."

"Seriously, no serious," Gabriel said. "I'm tired of serious. Serious needs a serious nap."

"You guys all heard Phillips," Dash said. He couldn't stop thinking about this, and needed to get it out. "He thinks we can't handle knowing what's actually going on with this mission. He said flat out he's going to keep more secrets from us."

"Have you ever *met* a grown-up?" Carly said. "They all think that way."

"Shawn only wants what is best for you," Chris said, trying to defend his friend.

"I know that," Dash admitted. "But what makes him think he *knows* what's best for us? Or at least, how does he know better than we do? Listen. We're the ones on this mission; we're the ones getting this done. Phillips doesn't know what it's really like out here. None of them back there do. We can't just trust the grown-ups to do our thinking for us. We need to trust our own judgment. Trust ourselves and each other. Uh . . ."

Dash felt his cheeks warm. He wasn't used to making grand speeches. He suddenly wondered whether this one had sounded inspiring or ridiculous. "Does that make sense?"

"One hundred percent," Carly said. "And I'm with you."

"We're all with you," Piper said. Gabriel agreed.

"Commander Phillips and I selected each member of this team for good reason," Chris said. "He trusted you to make the right decisions. I trust you too."

They looked at him expectantly, but Dash wasn't sure what it was they were expecting. "Um, okay, then, that's good," he said. "So, I guess, serious stuff officially concluded."

"Excellent," Gabriel said. "Now can we get back to what really matters? Like the fact that we're heading for *pirates*? Shiver me timbers! Ahoy, adventure!"

Carly looked at him like he was the alien. "You are so weird."

Gabriel narrowed his eyes at her. "No, you *aaaaargh*."

The others sighed. It was going to be a long three months.

Commander Shawn Phillips glared at the face on the monitor. He hated everything about it—the iron jaw, the narrow lips, the arrogant tilt of the brow. But most of all, he hated how much this face reminded him of his own.

"Father," he said, trying to keep his voice steady and confident. "We need to talk."

"No, son," Ike Phillips said. There was no warmth in his voice. No indication that they were anything but strangers to each other. "I don't think we do."

"You cloned Chris? You built a ship of your own and sent it after mine? You're trying to get the Source for yourself? Have you lost your mind?"

"You see? There's no need to talk, you've got all the answers. You've always been a sharp boy."

Shawn grimaced. No matter how old he got, his father could always make him feel like a silly child.

"What could you possibly think you're doing?" Shawn said. "Even I don't have an answer to that."

"And you don't need one," Ike Phillips said. "Look at you, all grown up and running a base of your own. Running a mission to save the planet. You probably thought I'd be proud of you. That I would respect you."

"I don't think about things like that," Shawn Phillips said. Which was a lie. That was the thing about having a man like Ike Phillips for a father. You never stopped wanting him to be proud of you. Or at least to respect you. But he never did.

He never would.

"You've been a great disappointment to me," his father said. "You and your little friend Chris too. But your sorry government mission has offered me an opportunity to achieve my goals, and for that, I suppose I should thank you."

"And what are those goals, Dad?" Shawn said, exasperated. He knew he'd never get a straight answer, but he couldn't help himself. He had to ask. "What exactly is it you want?"

"Why, I only want what I've always wanted," Ike Phillips said, as if surprised that Shawn hadn't caught on already. *"Everything."*

Later that night, Dash slipped into Chris's quarters to inject himself with the metabolism-freezing biologic. He should have been in a great mood—they'd retrieved the second element, they were well on their way to their next planet, things with Chris were finally settled—but he couldn't shake the black cloud hanging over him.

Finally, Chris called him on it. "Your treatment seems to be troubling you tonight," he said. "Are you experiencing symptoms? Or are you worrying about whether we'll complete the mission on time?"

"No," Dash said. "I mean, yeah, sure, I worry about that sometimes. No one will tell me exactly what happens if I'm out here too long, but it doesn't sound so good."

"Would you like me to tell you?" Chris asked.

Did he want that? Would it be better to know the details? Maybe all his hair and teeth would fall out; maybe his intestines would melt. Maybe he'd spontaneously combust, or simply vanish in a puff of smoke. These were the things that happened in his nightmares. He didn't particularly enjoy them—but on the other hand, he really didn't want to imagine the nightmares he might have if he knew for sure.

"Uh, not right now," Dash said. "And anyway, that's not really the problem. If I had a problem."

"Let's pretend you do," Chris said. "What might it be?"

"It's this," Dash said, gesturing toward the case of injectors. "I made this big deal about everyone having to be honest with each other, I got so mad at *you* for keeping this big secret—"

"I understood that," Chris interrupted. "You were right to be upset with me."

"Was I?" Dash said. "I can't tell anymore. Because aren't I keeping a huge secret from everyone, too? Should I tell them the truth?"

"Do you want to tell them the truth?" Chris asked.

"Yes? I mean, I want them to trust me. I want to deserve their trust. So, maybe? Well, no. I don't think so." Dash ran his hands through his hair. "I don't know."

"I can't tell you the answer, Dash. This is your life, your truth. It has to be your decision."

"Great," Dash muttered. Sometimes he got tired of making decisions. Sometimes he wished he *was* just a kid, and that there were some grown-ups around to tell him what to do.

"But I'm not sure I believe keeping some things private is the same as lying," Chris added. "And maybe trusting someone doesn't mean knowing every last thing about them. Maybe true trust means letting people make their own decision about how much to reveal. It's one of the things I like about human friendship. You believe in your friends—not because you know all the facts. But because you trust you know the ones that matter."

Dash thought about that moment back on Meta Prime, when he'd finally decided to accept Chris's help. There'd been so many reasons not to trust him, but Dash had done it anyway. And he'd been right.

"So you think maybe it's okay if I keep a secret or two for myself?" he asked.

"We all have secrets," Chris said, sounding almost sorry.

Dash left that night feeling really good for the first time since he'd landed on Meta Prime. He felt so good, in fact, that it didn't occur to him to wonder about the last thing Chris said.

Or about whatever it was he hadn't said.

Finally alone in his quarters for the night, Chris slid a small metal cube out from beneath his bed. It was the box he'd taken from planet J-16, having left it there for safekeeping several decades ago. As he'd done many nights before, he pried open the lid. Inside was evidence of his long journey: star charts, notes on the mineral content of planets across the galaxy, observations about the alien races he'd encountered. Everything he needed to help guide the Alpha team through the next several phases of their mission.

There was something else in the box.

Chris pulled out a small pouch and emptied the contents into his palm.

A smooth, polished stone that he had found by the sea when he was a small child.

Grains of the rust-red soil that surrounded his home on Flora.

A dried flower, its bright red and purple hues long since faded, that he'd been given by someone he loved.

A metal disk the size of a penny that, when activated, would project holographic images of anyone on Flora. It was the only way he could see the faces of the people he once knew.

Some days, it seemed like the only way he could remember them.

Chris pressed the disk into his palm but didn't activate it. He wasn't thinking about the friends he'd left behind, not tonight. He was thinking about the friends he had now, the friends on this ship, who thought they were all in this mission together. Who thought they knew what Chris really wanted.

He'd told the crew the truth: He wanted to help them achieve their mission. He wanted them to find all the elements, to synthesize the ultimate renewable energy source, to find their way back to Earth and save their planet.

But he hadn't told them the whole truth. He hadn't told them that the Source had another capability. That hidden away in a secret compartment of the *Cloud Leopard* was a much smaller ship—a ship that could be powered up with a small fraction of the Source.

It was Chris's ship. This mission was his chance—his only chance—to get back to Flora. He was keeping many secrets from Dash and the others, but this was the most important, and the most painful.

At the end of this journey, when the *Cloud Leopard* and the Alpha team returned to Earth, Chris wasn't going with them.

Chris was going home.

Find the Source. Save the world.

Follow the Voyagers to the next planet!

SIGN ON. JOIN THE CREW. SAVE THE WORLD!

VOYAGERS

3

OMEGA RISING

PATRICK CARMAN

Something about seeing Piper in the docking bay as the *Cloud Cat* prepared to lift off made Dash wonder if he'd made the right choice leaving her behind. Test scores didn't always determine the best person for the job; he'd learned that from personal experience. What had Chris said? *Don't underestimate what Piper can bring to this mission.*

"How would you guys feel about bringing Piper with us in the *Cloud Cat*?" Dash asked Carly and Gabriel. "I'd like to have her closer to the surface if something comes up."

"I thought we were going for an in-and-out extraction, nothing complicated," Carly reminded Dash.

"Yeah, totally. We are. But Chris and STEAM are already on the main ship. We've got them to navigate if we need to move the *Cloud Leopard*. Nothing's going to happen there. Why not bring her along, you know, just in case?"

Carly and Gabriel smirked at each other.

"What?" Dash asked.

"We knew this wasn't going to be as easy as you were hoping," Gabriel said. "Never is."

"Well, it should be quick and painless, but you're right, Gabriel," Dash admitted. "If there's one thing I'm learning out here, it's that things are always more complicated in real life than they are on a tablet."

"Especially in outer space," Carly added.

"Sure, bring Piper along for the ride," Gabriel said. "Can't hurt."

Dash felt good about the team again, confident and ready to roll.

"Hey, Piper!" Dash shouted down to the launch deck.

Looking up, Piper floated toward Dash, Rocket following her, barking excitedly. He was doing his canine best to wish them well.

"Chris and STEAM can manage things here," Dash said. "We need you with us."

Piper hesitated. Aqua Gen was a water planet, and she couldn't suddenly become a swimmer if things got out of control.

"You'll stay on the *Cloud Cat*," Dash said, reading her expression. "I just want you close by in case we need something. We'll position you right outside the atmosphere, where the AquaGens can't see you. STEAM could pick us up remotely, but you've gotten good at backup navigation. Better if we have a real person on deck."

In space—real outer space—Piper had fallen in love with navigation training almost as much as medicine. Gabriel and STEAM had put her through her paces on the long journey, and she'd mastered the *Cloud Cat* controls. She would never have the natural skills Gabriel had—he was off the charts—but she had to admit Dash was right.

Piper's apprehension seemed to fade away, and she drifted her air chair up the length of the ramp with Rocket close behind. The dog jumped into the *Cloud Cat* right behind Piper.

"Welcome aboard, Piper," Dash said. "And, uh, Rocket." Dash, Carly, Gabriel, and Piper exchanged a look, then laughed.

"It looks like this will be his first voyage to a distant planet, too," Carly said with a smile.

Rocket wagged his shaggy tail and barked.

"Ready to get this show on the road?" Gabriel asked.

Dash shook off what little nervousness remained and got down to the business of entering the world of Aqua Gen.

"Bring us in at zero mark fifty," Dash said. Gabriel had already plotted out their options and found a location entirely empty of life. No one on Aqua Gen would ever know they'd been visited by Voyagers.

"Zero mark fifty," Gabriel said, pushing the *Cloud*

Cat into high gear as it blasted away from the docking bay. The smaller ship wobbled under the power of its thrusters.

"Take it easy, Gabriel," Dash said. "Remember what Chris said: low profile."

But as usual, Gabriel was unable or unwilling to tone down his use of the Voyagers equipment. He was like a NASCAR driver; if Gabriel was behind the wheel of a race car with a track in front of him, there was only one choice—gun it.

"Bring us in about twenty feet from the surface," Dash said. "We'll deploy the watercraft first."

"I tested all the watercraft instruments in the premission phase," Carly said. "Best I can tell, everything checked out okay."

"It's a good thing we can't locate the element from up here," Gabriel said. "Otherwise we wouldn't have a chance to take those babies out for a spin."

The crew stopped talking as the ship accelerated. Dash gripped his armrests as his back pushed firmly into his seat. They were coming in hotter than Dash liked, nose down toward the watery surface of Aqua Gen.

"Pull back, Gabriel. You're heading in too steep."

"Oh, ye of little faith," Gabriel said as he expertly tilted the front of the *Cloud Cat*. They hovered precisely twenty feet above the surface of the water.

The pressure the crew felt subsided as soon as the ship leveled and slowed. Rocket, who had been sitting on Carly's lap, barked once with what Carly felt sure was appreciation.

"Piper, take the helm," Dash said.

Piper moved her air chair to a predetermined location at the front of the *Cloud Cat*. After Piper had cleared level nine navigation training, STEAM and a team of Zrks had retrofitted a locking hub for Piper to dock her chair. She settled in, and Rocket leapt from Carly's lap to sit obediently at Piper's side.

"I have the controls," Piper said, and she couldn't help smiling as she stared out at the serene surface of Aqua Gen.

The rest of the crew moved off the main deck and into the cargo hold at the rear. There Dash saw three personal watercraft and one submarine. The submarine was shaped like a twelve-foot torpedo, with two seats and controls that were dug into the center, like a kayak. It was a two-person vehicle, but the element extraction could be done with only one person. Dash planned to complete it himself, because it was more dangerous than he'd let on. There was nothing safe about finding yourself 20,000 feet under the surface of an endless sea. But the sub would need to wait; it was the watercraft they needed now.

Each watercraft was shaped like a wishbone, with a single seat positioned in the center of the Y. Propulsion came from the twin jet engines at the tail ends of the Y, and all the mapping tools were in the long nose. They were sleek, beautiful machines, cast in blue and green camouflage to match the surface.

"Man, I love this gig," Gabriel said as he stared at the most expensive watercraft ever created.

Carly was a bit more cautious than Gabriel. "It's too bad we can't send the sub in without this surface work," she said. "I don't like being exposed any longer than we have to."

Dash agreed, but they all knew the limitations of the technology. STEAM 6000 had made sure to explain it in excruciating detail and test them relentlessly while they were in Gamma Speed. They would need to ride the surface of the water and search for an oily film of Pollen Slither. Once they found that, they could trace a direct path to the source 20,000 feet below.

"If only the Pollen Slither wasn't so diluted when it reached the surface," Carly continued while they all put on life vests and boarded their own watercrafts.

"No way!" Gabriel said. "After all that training on the ship with these things, we've gotta ride 'em for real."

Dash knew he should reassure Carly, but he could feel himself being pulled into the gravitational force of Gabriel's excitement.

"I'm not going to lie. I have been looking forward to this."

"That's my man," Gabriel said, and he leaned out for a fist bump that Dash neglected to see.

"Don't leave me hangin'," Gabriel said.

Dash returned the bump, then turned to his left where Carly was seated and offered a fist bump to her. She took a deep, nervous breath and put on her helmet, ignoring Dash's fist. "Let's do this."

Dash and Gabriel put on their helmets, and they all buckled into their seats.

"Everyone ready?" Dash asked, testing the person-to-person audio inside the helmets. He got nods all around and tapped a command into his screen. "Piper, open bay doors."

"You got it," Piper said from the deck. A hydraulic sound filled the *Cloud Cat* bay, and light pierced Dash's eyes. He stared down a forty-five-degree metal ramp, followed by open air and water below. He tried to swallow and found a lump in his throat that felt like a walnut.

"Gabriel deploy in five, four, three, two, one," Dash ordered.

Gabriel's watercraft flew down the deck like a stone in a slingshot. It arced up and swayed left, then straightened out and glided onto the surface of the water. Gabriel zoomed out into the sea of Aqua Gen and circled back, waiting for the rest of his team as he pumped his fist in the air.

"Carly deploy in five—"

Dash didn't get any farther into the order before Carly's watercraft flew out of the cargo bay. She took a hard right and nearly flipped over, then went into a nosedive and pierced the surface, disappearing like a swordfish into the depths of Aqua Gen.

"Carly!" Dash yelled. Just as the water started to settle and turn smooth and glassy, Carly's watercraft burst out into the open again, achieved seven feet of amazing air, and landed perfectly on the surface.

Gabriel was super jealous.

"Aw, man, why didn't I think of that?" Gabriel said. "Incredible!"

"Thanks," Carly said. The audio on her helmet communication flickered, but she caught the end of what Gabriel was saying. She tried to smile, but she was soaking wet and a little bit shaken up. Then she thought about it: it *was* kind of a sweet move, and she was still breathing! Maybe this mission wasn't going to be so bad after all.

"Deploying now," Dash informed Piper. His finger was on the trigger that would send him hurtling onto an unknown planet. He hoped his landing would be more like Gabriel's than Carly's. "Close bay doors when I'm clear, then move point-seven-five miles off the surface and hold."

"Understood," Piper said. "And, Dash?"

"Yeah?"

"You're going to do great."

"Thanks, Piper."

Rocket barked his approval as well, and something about his decision to bring Piper along gave Dash the confidence he needed to press the button. He flew a straight path, hardly wobbling at all, and landed softly on the water below. Carly and Gabriel moved into formation beside him, and they all took a moment to gaze out over the endless liquid.

"We're on an alien planet, far away from home," Dash said.

"It never gets old," Gabriel added.

Carly didn't have any words. Mostly she felt relief—she'd done it. She was on another planet. A sun from another galaxy shone down on an aquamarine sea. She leaned over and looked into the endless depths, a void that seemed to go on forever.

The water darkened beneath her, and she looked overhead out of habit. Had a cloud drifted by, blotting out the sun? No, there were no clouds. When she looked back, it was gone. Or was it? Maybe all the water was darker beneath her.

"Did you guys see that?" she asked.

Carly couldn't be sure she'd seen anything, and she was concerned Dash and Gabriel already thought she was being too nervous. Maybe it was a trick of light from the shimmering sun.

"It was nothing, I think," Carly said.

Then she felt something bump against the bottom of her watercraft.

Dash looked to the sky, hoping to see the *Cloud Cat* still holding low to the water, but it was long gone. There was no time to call Piper back and complete the not-so-simple reboarding procedure. The water swelled up beneath him, like a blue whale was about to crest the surface. He felt the watercraft tilt to one side.

"Evacuate protocol one!" Dash yelled.

They'd practiced two types of evacuation plans during training. One meant stay together; two meant splitting apart and going in different directions. They'd practiced both in the event of an unexpected encounter during the extraction. It had taken all of a few seconds on Aqua Gen to stumble into something.

"Predator Z!" Dash yelled as he went straight to full throttle and the watercraft bucked and swayed beneath him. He looked back as the surface boiled higher, with Carly and Gabriel on the other side of the creature that was about to show itself.

Dash hoped his team had heard the order, but he couldn't be sure as the Predator Z broke the surface. It was like nothing Dash had ever seen or imagined, twice as big as a killer whale but so much faster. The length of its body flew into the air like a dolphin, dripping water beneath its great hull of a stomach. It was the most amazing shade of bright blue, which only made the rows of teeth stand out more.

Dash turned hard to the right, trying desperately to outrun the enormous wake the Predator Z created. A twenty-foot wall of water rose up behind him, pushing Dash faster and faster. The normal top speed of the watercraft was somewhere in the neighborhood of forty-five miles per hour, but the wave pushed his speed to sixty. He was flying along the surface, barely holding on.

Dash looked over one shoulder and then the other, but all he could see was the huge wave pushing him relentlessly away from Carly and Gabriel. He turned the watercraft softly to his left, preparing to try to make it over the cresting water. That was when he saw the Predator Z once more, its lizard-like skin just beneath the surface. It was moving as fast as Dash was, tracking him with a basketball-sized eye. A lightning bolt of fear shot through Dash's body as he throttled the watercraft to full speed, pulling away from the menacing eyeball. The beast moved in behind Dash and gave chase as Dash turned hard into the open sea and crouched down, becoming as aerodynamic as he could.

"Show me what you've got," he said as the watercraft sped up to seventy miles per hour. He'd seen footage of speedboats catching the wrong angle and going airborne, tumbling end over end and breaking into pieces. One wrong move and the same fate awaited Dash, and then he'd be Predator Z food for sure. The water was an endless sheet of glass in front of him, and he glided along its surface in a perfectly straight line. A full minute passed and he didn't look back. It felt to Dash like he could keep searching for a distant shore forever.

At last he risked lifting his head and turning around, expecting to see the great alien creature of the sea bearing down on him. Instead he saw only the wake he'd left behind, like the third-base line to home. He slowed down, then came to a stop, bobbing gently on the water.

"Where are you?" he whispered, searching every inch of the horizon.

Dash doubled back to look for his teammates, hoping they hadn't been capsized. He saw nothing. No Predator Z. No Carly or Gabriel. He drove the watercraft in a circle, feeling a sudden loss of direction. Everything looked the same. Water, water, and more water.

"Carly! Gabriel!" he called out. He was alone on a planet far from home, and the quiet unnerved him. He felt a loneliness he hadn't experienced for weeks. On his second spin around, Dash saw the Predator Z rise once more, about a hundred yards to his left. It was cutting a path in the distance, and he felt a pang of hysteria at the idea that one or both of his friends were clutched between its teeth.

Dash double-checked the helmet communication system and tried again.

"Gabriel, come in! Carly, answer!"

Silence.

Robin Wasserman is the bestselling author of several books for children and young adults, including the Chasing Yesterday trilogy, the Cold Awakening trilogy, *The Book of Blood and Shadow*, and *The Waking Dark*. Her books have sold more than half a million copies, appeared on many best-of-year lists, and been adapted into a television miniseries. She grew up in the Philadelphia suburbs, where, in the grand tradition of the only child, she told herself stories to pass the time. Now she lives in Brooklyn, New York, and is still telling herself stories. The only difference is that now she writes them down for other people to read (and that she's allowed to eat dessert for dinner). She's still hoping to be the first woman on Mars. Or, at least, once she's very old, to move to a nice retirement village on the moon.

Find out more at robinwasserman.com.

Ready for more kids saving the world?

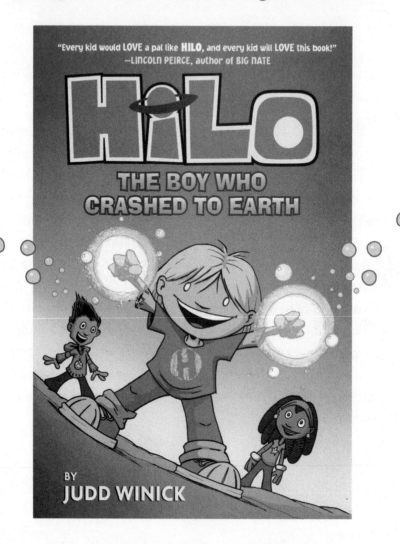

"**Fast paced**, furiously **funny**, and will have kids waiting on the edge of their seats. **Aaaaaaaaaahhhh!**"
—JEFFREY BROWN, author of *Jedi Academy*

"Every kid would **LOVE** a pal like **HILO**, and every kid will love this book!"
—LINCOLN PEIRCE, author of *Big Nate*

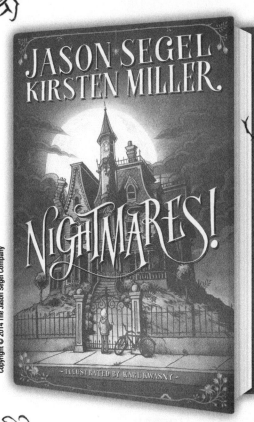

VOYAGERS

Don't miss a single Voyage. . . .

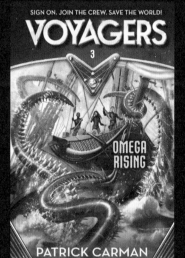

REPORT TO BASE TEN

MISSION BRIEFING

ATTENTION: AUTHORIZED PERSONNEL ONLY

All team members are required to check in for tactical training and deep-space ZRK probe operations IMMEDIATELY. Your participation is critical to the success of our mission.

- CRACK the book codes
- JOIN Top-Secret Missions
- BUILD your own ZRK Commander
- EXPLORE the depths of space
- EARN badges, unlock rewards, and level up

DIGITAL GAMING EXPERIENCE
UNLOCKS FALL 2015